SHOWTYM ADVENTURES

KOOLIO,
THE PROBLEM PONY

THIS BOOK BELONGS TO:

_____

_____

Also in this series:

DANDY,
THE MOUNTAIN PONY

CAMEO,
THE STREET PONY

CASPER,
THE SPIRITED ARABIAN

CHESSY,
THE WELSH PONY

KELLY WILSON

SHOWTYM ADVENTURES

KOOLIO, THE PROBLEM PONY

PUFFIN

UK | USA | Canada | Ireland | Australia
India | New Zealand | South Africa | China

Puffin is an imprint of the Penguin Random House group of companies, whose addresses
can be found at global.penguinrandomhouse.com.

Penguin
Random House
New Zealand

First published by Penguin Random House New Zealand, 2019

10 9 8 7 6 5 4 3 2 1

Design by Emma Jakicevich © Penguin Random House New Zealand
Author photo by Amanda Wilson
Illustrations by Heather Wilson © Penguin Random House New Zealand
Cover illustration by Jenny Cooper © Penguin Random House New Zealand

Printed and bound in Australia by Griffin Press, an Accredited ISO AS/NZS 14001
Environmental Management Systems Printer

A catalogue record for this book is available from the National Library of New Zealand.

ISBN 978-0-14-377226-2
eISBN 978-0-14-377227-9

penguin.co.nz

This book is dedicated to everyone who has helped us along on our equestrian journey. We wouldn't be where we are today without the wisdom you shared with us over the years. Thank you.

Growing up, we Wilson sisters — Vicki, Amanda and me (I'm Kelly) — were three ordinary girls with a love of horses and dreams of Grand Prix show jumping, taming wild horses and becoming world champions.

In *Showtym Adventures*, we want to share stories based on our early years with ponies, to inspire you to have big dreams, too! I hope you enjoy reading about the special ponies that started us on our journey...

Love,
  Kelly

Contents

Chapter 1
Truck Troubles

"WE HAVE TOO MANY PONIES," Dad announced. The Wilson family was gathered around the kitchen table, reading over the calendar of events for the upcoming season and highlighting all the horse shows they wanted to attend. They all looked up at him with surprise.

"We only have five ponies at the moment," eleven-year-old Kelly laughed.

"Lucky we found homes for all the wild Welsh ponies," her little sister Amanda added. "Only a couple of months ago we had nine on the property!"

"What I *should* have said is that our horse truck is too small," Dad clarified. "Last season we had to make two trips to get all of the ponies to the local shows, but we can't keep doing that forever. With Cameo, Dandy, Casper and Magic all performing so well, it seems a shame one has to be left behind every weekend."

"You're right, three spaces isn't enough," Mum said thoughtfully. "And there have been plenty of times when I've wished I could join you girls for a beach ride, but we couldn't fit Jude in. You're lucky I don't compete, otherwise we'd really be fighting for spots in the truck."

Kelly looked over at her older sister. While Kelly always rode her mare, Cameo, Vicki had *two* ponies, which meant that one often had to be left behind. But both were very special, and Kelly didn't envy Vicki having to choose between them. Dandy, a chestnut who'd been with their family for four years, had run wild in the mountains before coming to their family, and Casper the grey Arabian had been aggressive and badly misunderstood when they'd saved him a year earlier. Now both were well trained, and thirteen-year-old Vicki had won many Champions with them.

"So I guess we need a bigger truck, then." Vicki's eyes sparkled as she said this, and Kelly guessed that she was imagining all the ribbons she could win if both Casper and Dandy were able to go to all the shows.

Dad nodded in agreement, though his expression was grave. "I've been thinking about that for a while, but there's no way we would have enough money selling our current truck to upgrade to a bigger one. Even with some money saved up from selling Charlie and the Welsh ponies, we just can't afford it."

"Can we earn the extra money?" Kelly asked. Over the past few years they'd often given pony rides, sold horse manure or made show browbands and rope halters to raise funds for new ponies or gear, when money was short. "You know we're not afraid of hard work."

Eight-year-old Amanda shuffled forward in her seat, eager to help, too. "We could sell some of our baby rabbits, and the canaries and finches that just hatched."

"We wouldn't just need a couple of hundred dollars, though." Dad sighed. "It'd be thousands and thousands of dollars, and the sooner the better, so we could use the new truck this season."

"Can't you just have one pony, Vicki?" Amanda said. The youngest in the family, and always full of energy, she was already tired of this conversation. "Everyone would fit if you sold either Casper or Dandy."

Vicki glanced at her sister in horror. "They're my best friends! I'd rather stop competing than sell them!"

"It's important that all of you can compete, as much as our finances allow," Mum said soothingly. "We know you girls love the horses, and we want to help support your dreams. We just have to find a way to afford a bigger truck."

Around the table everyone fell silent, thinking through options.

"I should sell Jude," Mum said finally, in a resolute voice. "I'm so busy helping you girls with your ponies, I barely have time to work mine anymore. I'm lucky if I ride once a week at the moment."

"It'd be a good start, but I still don't know if it would bring in enough money," Dad said. "Jude has only done trekking, so she wouldn't be worth as much as the girls' competition ponies."

"So we sell two?" Kelly suggested quietly.

"Magic's only on lease, so it can't be Amanda's pony," Mum said as she stood up to help set the table. "Which only leaves Cameo, Casper and Dandy. I can't imagine either of you wanting to part with any one of those three!"

Kelly's eyes widened at the thought of her beautiful steel-grey mare being sold. She hurriedly shook her head. "I guess I didn't think that through very well. There's no way I'd ever sell Cameo!"

Dad turned to his eldest daughter and raised an eyebrow. "Vicki?"

Vicki shook her head adamantly. "There's no point having a five-horse truck if we have no ponies to put in it. It'd break my heart to part with either of my ponies."

"But if we don't upgrade the truck, you girls will always be limited to competing one pony each at the shows. That will stifle how much experience you can gain," Dad said, eyeing first Vicki, then Kelly and Amanda. "If you are all serious about riding, then the more you can ride and compete the better."

"So what's the answer?" Kelly asked, getting up to check on the lasagne she had prepared. She'd made a deal with her parents a few months earlier that she could skip her turn washing the dishes each week if she cooked instead. "Maybe we should just alternate ponies for each show like we did last year?"

But all the same she couldn't help but agree with her father. Horse riding was like any skill — the more hours you spent practising something, the faster you improved. For Vicki especially, who had dreams of competing against the best riders in the world, having two horses at each show would double her time in the saddle.

U U U

"I think I have a solution," Mum said later that evening, long after they had finished Kelly's tasty lasagne. "I'll sell Jude, that's a given. Then we'll also advertise the other three ponies we own. The first one to find a buyer will go, and we'll keep the other two. I think it's the fairest way, without having to choose between them."

Kelly gasped and almost dropped the book she was reading. "But what if it's Cameo? That wouldn't be fair! I'll have no pony to ride, and Vicki will still have two."

"I'll be just as devastated if either Casper or Dandy are sold," Vicki said, her eyes wide. "Surely we can come up with another plan?"

"I'd understand if Magic had to be sold. I'd be sad, for sure, but I'd be OK with it," Amanda whispered, feeling the tension between her sisters.

"But you've only been leasing her for a few months," Vicki said dismissively. "And for half the time you didn't even like her. It's different for Kelly and me — Cameo, Casper and Dandy are part of the family."

"In the past we've always banded together when we've needed something new, and both Dad and I think this is important," Mum said. "We lived in tents for almost a year when we first moved north, because we didn't have enough money left over after buying land to build a house."

"And remember when Vicki had to ride bareback on Bella for months, because we couldn't afford a new saddle?" Dad said. His expression was serious as he looked at the girls. "Sometimes it's not about what we *want* to do, but about what we *need* to do.

This family doesn't back away from sacrifices and struggles if we have our goal in sight."

"But it's taken so long to train up our ponies to be capable of winning at a high level." Vicki frowned. "It'll put us back years if we have to start from scratch with a green pony."

"You are all better riders now," Mum said. "And we'll be able to pay a little extra for a more experienced pony. Whoever's pony sells can have a thousand dollars to spend on a new one, and the rest will go towards a new truck."

"A thousand dollars!" Kelly gasped. She was unable to comprehend spending that much. "But all our ponies cost no more than three hundred."

Mum smiled. "That was before you girls did such a good job of training them. Now they are worth a lot more. So, after we've sold two ponies, we'll be able to find a nice young one without too many issues, so it won't take so long to get it ready to compete."

As Kelly prepared for bed that night, she was filled with dread. She found training ponies scary — it had taken a long time for her to trust Cameo, and she couldn't imagine having to begin all over again with another inexperienced pony. She could only hope that someone would buy one of Vicki's ponies first, but even that thought made her heart hurt.

"No matter which pony gets sold, there's not going to be a happy ending," Kelly sighed when her parents came to tuck them into bed.

"Not straight away," her mum agreed. "It's always hard saying goodbye, but eventually there will come a time when we'll all be thankful for a bigger truck."

Chapter 2
Up For Sale

By LATE SEPTEMBER, Jude had been sold for $2500 to a local family who wanted a pony for trekking. Although Mum was sad to see her go, she was very happy with Jude's new home. The hardest part for Kelly and Vicki, though, was knowing they might have to part with one of their own ponies soon.

Because Cameo, Casper and Dandy were worth twice as much as Jude, rather than being advertised locally they were listed in the *Horse Trader* magazine, so people all around the country could look at them.

From the moment the magazine hit the shelves on the first of the month, the phone didn't stop ringing. Dandy, with all of his successes, was a firm favourite with riders wanting a versatile competition pony, while Cameo was popular with parents whose kids needed a safe and dependable all-rounder. Soon they had people from all over New Zealand and some from overseas lined up to visit them.

"I'm glad there's not as much interest in Casper," Vicki said after they'd taken yet another phone call about Dandy. "He had so many issues when he first arrived, I'd feel so guilty if he ended up confused and misunderstood again."

Kelly bit her lip. "Cameo and Dandy would be OK with a new owner though, right?"

Uncertainty clouded Vicki's expression. "I think Cameo would be fine — she is so calm she would be perfect for anyone. But I'm worried about Dandy. I'm the only one who's really handled or ridden him since he got mustered from the mountains. I'm not sure how he'd cope suddenly having to adapt to a new home, with total strangers."

"Isn't someone coming to look at him next weekend?" Kelly asked. She felt for Vicki, but was also glad that it wasn't Cameo who was being tried first.

Vicki nodded, clearly trying to keep a brave face. "The family from Tahiti want to try him on Saturday. Then another girl is coming to view Cameo on Sunday."

U U U

Saturday came and went, and although the young Tahitian girl loved Dandy, her family wanted time to try other ponies and consider all their options. Vicki's relief was obvious as she led her beloved pony back to his paddock, but she gave Kelly a sympathetic look as she passed.

The night before Cameo's potential buyers arrived, Kelly lay awake. She'd always thought that she and Cameo were the most perfectly matched pair in the whole world. But what if this girl also thought Cameo was perfect for *her*?

Giving up on sleep, she slipped out of bed. Pausing to check that her sisters were still fast asleep, she crept out of the room and down the hallway, and let herself outside. Then, knowing the way by heart, she ran through the darkness to Cameo's paddock.

"Come on, girl," Kelly called softly to her.

The steel-grey mare wandered over, the white highlights on her coat glowing in the moonlight. Just as she always did, she pushed her head into Kelly's arms for a hug.

"She's going to love you," Kelly whispered.

She threaded her hands through Cameo's mane and jumped onto her pony's bare back. For more than an hour she sat quietly on her pony, watching the sky for shooting stars. Finally, when she had become so tired that her eyes would barely stay open, she slid to the ground, patted Cameo, who blinked sleepily in reply, and made her way back to bed.

U U U

The next morning, Kelly woke late and stumbled into the kitchen. No one else was around. She glanced at the clock and gasped — it was almost 11 o'clock! The family looking at Cameo were due any minute.

"Good to see you've joined the land of the living," Dad joked as Kelly came running out to the yards.

Vicki already had Cameo caught and groomed. "We were beginning to think we'd have to meet these people without you."

"They're not here yet, are they?"

Vicki shook her head. "They've called to say they're running a little late. Would you like me to ride Cameo for them today?"

Kelly shot her a grateful smile. "Maybe you should, and then I can get to know the girl who's trying her. She has to be good enough for Cameo. Besides, I'll probably cry the whole time if I'm the one who has to show her off."

At that moment, a car pulled up. As her parents spoke with the family, Kelly looked hard for any faults, but they seemed friendly and genuine. Their daughter was ten years old and they were looking for a safe all-rounder for her. If they bought Cameo, she would stay in the family for years, passing to their younger daughter, who was already trading jokes and giggling with Amanda.

Once Vicki had put Cameo through her paces, the ten-year-old wanted to try riding her. Kelly watched in misery as her pony behaved impeccably. The girl brought Cameo to a halt with a radiant smile, and it was clear to everyone that she was smitten.

Kelly clung to Cameo's neck as the girl's parents again talked with her mum and dad. Tears began to trickle down her cheeks. In an effort to hide her heartbreak, she led Cameo back to her paddock, where she stayed for a while, sitting with her back leaning against the trunk of a tree.

Back at the house she was greeted with sympathetic looks.

"They've bought her, haven't they?"

Mum nodded and put an arm around Kelly's shoulder. "It'll be a good home for her; they'll treat her well."

"When does she go?"

"Next weekend. They live near Granny, so we'll drive Cameo there ourselves and stay with Granny for the weekend . . ." Mum's voice faded out as the news sank in for Kelly.

Just one week left with Cameo.

Blinking rapidly, Kelly rushed to her room and flung herself on the bed.

The week passed far too quickly and Kelly walked around in a daze. Every morning she woke early to spend time with Cameo, then she'd yawn her way through school before hurrying home and riding in the evenings. To make the most of her final days with Cameo, Kelly and her sisters revisited some of their favourite rides. On Monday they rode to the dairy and got lollies, on Tuesday they cantered around the neighbours' farm, on Wednesday they jumped in the front paddock, and on Thursday they rode to the reserve and played tag on horseback.

A few times, Mum and Vicki tried to raise Kelly's spirits by pointing out ponies for sale in the local newspaper and magazines. But Kelly was unable to bear the thought of replacing Cameo.

"It wouldn't be fair," she said. "None of them would measure up."

"You'll have to start trying ponies at some point," Mum encouraged her. "Getting over Cameo will be easier if you have a new pony to focus on."

Kelly turned away. "I will," she muttered as she headed outside to feed the animals. "Eventually."

Chapter 3
The Saddest Goodbye

ON FRIDAY AFTERNOON, the sisters were picked up from school in the horse truck. Cameo wasn't the only pony making the five-hour drive south — Dandy and Magic were also joining them. The plan was to spend all day Saturday at the beach with the ponies, then deliver Cameo to her new home on Sunday.

As they drove, Kelly distracted herself by joining in the family games. First they played "I Spy", followed by "Twenty Questions" and then "Spot the Animals". Along country roads they kept a keen eye out — the winner would be the first person to find ten cows, ten sheep, five horses, two dogs, one donkey (or a yellow car) and a goat (or a purple car).

"That's my goat!" Dad cried out, pointing to a purple car parked on the side of the road.

Amanda huffed in exasperation. "I only needed a donkey!"

They arrived at their granny's house in the dark, jumping out of the car to hug her with excitement. They hadn't seen her for more than a year, and the girls couldn't wait to fill her in on everything that had been happening.

U U U

The next morning, Mum woke them before dawn, and they drove down to the beach to watch the sunrise. It was Mum's favourite place in the world, and even though the water was cold, she convinced them to join her for a swim.

"It's freezing!" Kelly shrieked as she dashed into the waves and ducked under the water just long enough to get wet before sprinting back out. Vicki and Amanda weren't far behind her, and they quickly wrapped themselves in towels.

As they made their way back to the car, Vicki saw some wooden barriers along the estuary that were used to stop the banks of the reserve from eroding away.

"They would make awesome jumps! We should bring our ponies down and ride while the tide's low enough to jump them."

Kelly looked at the eight barriers, which jutted out, one after another, towards the channel. At their lowest point, at the edge of the water, they were just 30 centimetres high, but against the grass bank they were almost 1 metre.

"Cameo will love it," she said, before remembering that it would be their very last ride together. Not wanting to ruin their last day, though, she shook away the depressing thought and ran to catch up to her sisters.

After a quick breakfast, they caught their ponies and rode bareback to the beach, with their parents following behind on foot. As soon as they reached the estuary, Kelly and her sisters cantered their ponies, hooves pounding in the sand. When the barriers came into view, they were relieved to see the tide was still low enough to give them plenty of room to jump.

Kelly took the lead, aiming for the middle of each barrier. Over each jump Cameo soared, fitting several strides between each one. Behind her Vicki

and then Amanda followed, clutching their ponies' manes so they wouldn't slip off their bare backs.

"Let's do it again!" Vicki cried out as they landed over the final barrier.

Circling Cameo around, Kelly headed back the way they had come, this time aiming for the highest

end. As she pulled Cameo up at the far end of the estuary, she reached down to hug her pony's neck.

"I'm going to miss her terribly," Kelly said to her sisters as they made their way back to their mum and dad.

"That's what you said when you had to sell Twinkle, too," Vicki reminded her in an attempt to lighten her mood. "But I bet you can't imagine riding a pony that small anymore. Maybe you'll enjoy the challenge of training a new pony."

Though she was highly doubtful, Kelly kept quiet. She wanted to savour her final moments on Cameo. As they all made their way back down the road to their granny's house, memories flashed through her mind: the first moment she'd seen Cameo, the time when she, Vicki and Amanda had tripled on her at a Ribbon Day, and when she'd competed Cameo at her first Royal Easter Show. By the time Kelly dismounted, a small, sad smile had once again crept onto her face. She would miss Cameo, but she'd never forget all the fun they'd had.

The next morning, they took Cameo to her new home. The new family were lining the driveway when they arrived, and their obvious excitement was in stark contrast to Kelly's sombre mood.

Putting on a brave face, she jumped out of the truck and unloaded her beloved pony for the last time to lead her towards the stables. As they walked down the driveway a gorgeous chestnut pony, who had been resting under a towering oak tree, nickered out and trotted over to meet them.

"That's Oscar — he'll be Cameo's new paddock mate," the younger of the two girls said. This was the last straw — Kelly's heart broke at the thought that Cameo was not only losing all the people she knew, but also all the ponies she'd come to know since arriving at their property two years earlier.

"Do you think she'll miss Dandy, Casper and Magic very badly?" Kelly asked her mother through quivering lips.

"I think she'll miss them for a little bit," Mum replied, nodding sympathetically. "But I bet she'll enjoy having Oscar for company."

They soon reached the stables, which were beautiful, and looked out over a huge arena dotted with brightly coloured jumps. Kelly gasped when she saw Cameo's name was already engraved on the door. She was awed by how pretty everything was. Cameo's new home was so different to their own mismatched collection of sheds and yards.

All too soon it was time to say goodbye. Kelly clung to Cameo for as long as possible.

"Come on, Kelly," Mum said gently. "We've got a long drive ahead of us."

Reluctantly, Kelly stroked Cameo's head for the last time. The mare nickered in reply. With tears welling in her eyes she sprinted to the truck, crawling into the back so she could have some privacy. As her dad started the engine and drove down the steep, long driveway, Kelly couldn't stop the sobs wracking her body. Saying goodbye to Cameo was one of the hardest things she'd ever had to do.

Chapter 4
In Search of a Pony

IN THE DAYS THAT FOLLOWED, Kelly threw herself into her schoolwork to keep herself distracted. A new truck had to be bought, with the money from selling Charlie and the Welsh ponies and from the sales of Jude and Cameo. Even so, all they could afford was an empty shell, which Dad immediately set about converting, adding accommodation and a ramp.

In spite of the hole left by Cameo's departure, Kelly began to realise that she was badly missing riding, especially when she had to watch from the sidelines as her sisters competed at the first Ribbon Day of the season. If there was to be any chance of her being able to compete before Christmas, she had to start looking for a new pony — and soon.

Picking up the latest *Horse Trader* magazine, which Mum kept leaving about the house to tempt her, Kelly began to look at all the photos of ponies for sale. She circled her favourites on every page, gasping at their prices. She had thought a thousand dollars was a lot, but it wouldn't go very far at all, she now realised. Still, she had to work with the amount that her parents had promised her, so she quickly flipped through to the "$1000 and Under" section. Here only a few words described each pony, and there were no photos. Most of them sounded old, or difficult, and Kelly quickly scanned through the listings. Finally, one caught her eye. She paused, re-reading the ad.

Stunning six-year-old 146-centimetre grey gelding. Huge promise for a talented young rider wanting to produce a top competition prospect. $1000.

Running down to the front paddock, Kelly found her mum watching Amanda and Vicki jumping their ponies. Shoving the magazine in front of her mother, Kelly pointed to the listing.

"Can we ring up about this one?" she asked breathlessly.

A relieved smile crossed Mum's face. "Your sisters have just finished riding, so let's head inside and call them right now."

Kelly dashed back to the house and waited nervously for her mother to catch up. A pony this promising would be snapped up quickly, and she couldn't be sure that another would come along. What if they missed out? As she re-read the ad, she felt a twinge of sadness over Cameo. But no matter how much she wished for it, Cameo wasn't coming back. It was time to focus on the future and find a new pony so she could start riding again.

"Am I ringing, or would you like to?" Mum asked as she came inside.

"You can — you'll know all the right questions to ask," Kelly said, bouncing as she sat on the edge of a kitchen chair.

For the next few minutes Kelly listened to the

one-sided conversation, trying to imagine what the owners were saying about their pony. From her mum's comments she learned the pony was named Koolio, and that he lived about ten hours' drive away.

"Tell me everything about him," Kelly pleaded as soon as Mum hung up the phone.

"He's only young and quite inexperienced," Mum began slowly, "but the owner is confident that with the right rider he could be one of the best ponies in the country."

"Then why are you talking like there is something wrong? He sounds like my dream pony!" Kelly exclaimed.

"It's just that he's so far away," Mum sighed. "But then the owner said she's competing at a Three-Day Event this weekend and it's only half the distance from here. If we're able to drive down to meet her at the event, she'll bring him along for us to try."

"Is he competing there?" Kelly said.

"No, not competing — apparently he's never been to a show in his life. But you'd be able to ride him around the showgrounds."

"Try who?" Vicki asked, as she and Amanda appeared in the doorway, kicking off their boots.

"Kelly's finally found a pony she wants to try," Mum said. "He just happens to be at the opposite end of the North Island. But if we drop everything this weekend, we might be able to meet him halfway. I need to talk to your father and see if he's willing to make the trip, and then call the owner back."

"So we're going on another road trip?" Amanda squealed in delight. "So what's so special about this pony, anyway?"

Kelly's grin faded — she realised she really didn't know much about Koolio.

"I have a good feeling about him — and Mum said he sounded really promising when she spoke to his owner on the phone." She shrugged as she passed over the magazine so her sisters could read the brief description.

"Why him, of all the ponies?" Vicki asked.

"I'm not sure why he stood out," Kelly admitted. "There's not even a photo."

"Well, it might have been the price," Vicki said with a wink, and began flicking through the rest of the magazine, pausing to read an interview with one of the country's leading riders. "I've always wanted to try eventing," she said.

"I thought you were stuck on showing or show jumping," Mum laughed. "I can never keep up with you!"

"Maybe we'll do a little bit of everything," Vicki grinned as she held out the magazine. "This interview with Mary Campbell sure makes eventing sound fun."

Mum's eyebrows rose as she glanced down at the open page. "I'm pretty sure she's the owner of Koolio I've just been speaking to!"

"We have to go try him, then," Kelly said. "Even if we don't end up buying him, it'd be great to watch the event, and meet one of New Zealand's top riders in person."

U U U

That evening, after Kelly and her sisters had cleaned their gear and fed all their animals, they headed inside. It was always hard to fit everything in on school days, and often the sun had set long before they were finished. Today was no exception.

"You're in late again," Dad said as they settled

down at the table, where Mum was laying out a roast dinner.

Amanda nodded. "We spent ages playing with our rabbits and guinea pigs, then checked the aviary to make sure all the baby birds were OK."

"How are they doing?"

"Another finch had fallen out of the nest, so we put it back with the others," Kelly said. "I hope they all make it."

"With you three to care for them, they'll have a better chance than most," Mum said, as she took a seat. "Right — Dad and I have been talking about driving down to see Koolio."

Kelly eyed her parents in anticipation.

"We've rung Mary, and she's going to bring him up for you to try at the show this weekend. We'll leave at 4 a.m. on Saturday, so we can watch some of the cross country, too."

"Really?" Kelly gasped, unable to believe it was all happening so fast.

"Truly," Dad confirmed. "And we'll take the horse truck. If you decide you like him, there's no way we're making that drive twice!"

Chapter 5
Dream Pony

TWO DAYS LATER, Kelly was woken from a deep sleep. Sitting up, for a brief second she didn't know where she was. And then it hit her: last night she and her sisters had gone to bed in the horse truck so they would be able to sleep through the wee hours of the morning on their drive south to try out Koolio.

Kelly heard the cab door shutting, and looked out the window to see why they'd stopped. Excitement filled her as the truck rumbled to life again and they turned into the driveway of the showgrounds, which led past hundreds of yards filled with horses.

"We're here!" she cried, jiggling her sisters awake.

Vicki joined her at the window. "I can't wait to watch the cross country."

"Me, too," Kelly yawned. "But mostly I can't wait to meet Koolio!"

"And I can't believe we slept the whole way," Amanda said, rubbing her eyes.

∪ ∪ ∪

An hour later the girls were wide awake, sitting on the hill overlooking the water jump. A crowd had gathered to watch the country's best riders navigate the challenging set of jumps. Already they'd seen two riders fall, their horses galloping off as they emerged from the murky water.

"We'd better head back," Mum said, glancing at her watch. "Mary's meeting us at the warm-up arena in twenty minutes."

Kelly leapt up eagerly. She'd been waiting for this moment for days, and now that it was finally here she didn't want to be late.

"Can't we watch a couple more?" Vicki begged, her

eyes locked on a chestnut mare jumping the course.

Mum shook her head. "Mary is fitting us in between her rounds — we can't keep her waiting."

Detouring past their truck, Kelly pulled on her helmet and boots, then followed her family between the long lines of imposing horse trucks. In every direction horses were being led, washed, saddled or ridden. Like she had all morning, since they had arrived, she kept her eyes peeled for a grey pony.

"Do you think that's him?" Kelly asked, pointing to a dark grey gelding prancing along the track, tugging at the reins.

"He's way too big!" Vicki laughed.

"What about that one?" Amanda said, pointing to a much smaller grey, with a steel-grey mane and tail and dapples on its legs.

Kelly whipped her head around to see, and her mouth fell open as she caught sight of the beautiful pony who stood at the gate of the warm-up arena. The young woman holding his reins lifted a hand in greeting. In that moment, Kelly knew he was meant for her.

"He's stunning," she breathed as she walked up to the gate and held up a hand to pat him. Pulling away from her touch, Koolio eyed her warily and cocked an ear.

"Oh, don't mind him — he takes a while to get used to new people," the woman grinned. "I'm Mary, by the way, and this is Koolio."

After they had all made their introductions, Mary hopped on Koolio and put him through his paces for the family. He was a little spooky and unsettled, but there was no doubting it — he was stunning. After they'd seen him walk, trot and canter, Kelly watched in awe as he jumped over the practice fences. Although obviously inexperienced, he was more talented than she could possibly have dreamed.

"Would you like to have a ride on him?" Mary asked, riding Koolio over to them.

Unable to speak, Kelly bobbed her head vigorously. The stirrup length was adjusted and Kelly was legged up into the saddle. Beneath her, the powerful grey shifted around uneasily, and Kelly glanced nervously at the ground. All of a sudden it looked awfully far away, and she found her confidence draining away with it. She took a deep breath and reminded herself that she had become a much better rider since she'd first got Cameo.

"He's much bigger than I'm used to," Kelly said as Koolio stamped a hoof impatiently.

"He's a little on edge from being in an unfamiliar environment," Mary said, rubbing Koolio between the eyes. "But this is about the worst he gets."

"I thought he looked great." Kelly let out a deep breath and rolled her shoulders, trying to calm herself. "He's a really good jumper."

"He's going to be amazing once he gets a little more mileage," Mary agreed. "Let's get you out on a circle so you can get used to the feel of him."

Soon Kelly was trotting around the arena, listening to Mary's instructions. Although half her attention was focused on the lesson, the rest of the time she found herself daydreaming about all the Champions she could win with a pony as gorgeous as Koolio.

"That's great," Mary called out, jolting Kelly back to reality. "Keep that trot and approach the crossbar."

Unlike Cameo, who had been steady and reliable, Koolio felt hesitant and wobbly beneath Kelly, and nerves filled her as she approached the jump. Shortening her reins to keep him straight, Kelly urged him forward, and Koolio jumped awkwardly.

Caught off balance, Kelly pulled sharply on the reins as he landed and bit back a cry of alarm.

"Try again — just keep your hands a little softer," Mary called out.

Kelly took a deep breath and circled Koolio before approaching the jump again. This time Koolio did a massive jump and Kelly stood in the stirrups, sliding her hands up his neck to give him plenty of rein.

"Ready for something bigger?" Mary asked, bending over to raise the poles from a crossbar into an upright.

"Is it all right if we stop now?" Kelly asked, turning to her parents. "I really, really like him, but he's much faster and more inexperienced than I'm used to. I think it will be a few weeks before I'll feel confident jumping any bigger."

"You're riding him really well," Mary assured her. "He's going exactly the right speed for a pony of his size. If you've been riding a smaller pony, it'll take a few rides before you adjust to the length of his stride."

"Really?" Kelly said, leaning over to pat Koolio's neck. "He feels really fast to me."

"I know he's a big step up, but you look good

on him," Mum said. "Remember when you changed from Twinkle to Cameo — you thought she was much bigger and faster, too."

"How about just one upright before you finish?" Dad suggested.

"Just a small one," Kelly agreed reluctantly. Although his trot and canter were much bigger than Cameo's, she knew that Koolio hadn't actually done anything wrong.

Picking up a trot, she turned towards the jump for the last time. Not only was the height of the jump worrying her, she was also anxious about riding in front of Mary.

But as the jump loomed closer, her nerves faded away. All too soon they were airborne. Up and up Koolio soared, before landing neatly on the other side of the fence. Although the jump was only about 60 centimetres, it felt as though they had jumped much higher. Kelly couldn't contain the grin that spread across her face.

"It might take me a while to get used to him, but he's my dream pony in every way," she announced as she rode over to join her family at the rail. She noticed the slightly dazed expressions on her sisters' faces.

"He cleared that jump by miles," Vicki said, shaking her head in disbelief.

"Am I right in guessing he'll be coming home with us?" Mum grinned.

"Yes, please!" Kelly whooped. She jumped down off the grey gelding and gave him a hug. This felt like the beginning of something great.

Chapter 6
Spooked

A COUPLE OF DAYS LATER, Kelly got Koolio ready for their first ride at home. He had been a little difficult to catch and then, to her shock, he'd tried to bite and kick her while she was undoing the straps on his cover. As she put on the saddle he still seemed unsettled. This was not getting off to the start Kelly had hoped for with the pony of her dreams.

Standing on tiptoe, she reached up to bridle him. Unlike Cameo, who had always snuggled up to her, Koolio stood aloof as she worked with him.

"Are you a little shy around strangers?" Kelly

asked her new pony, as she swung the reins over his head and prepared to hop on his back.

Vicki, who was saddling up Casper, glanced over. "I'm sure once he gets to know you he'll relax."

"Hopefully that doesn't take too long," Kelly sighed, swinging herself up into the saddle. "The next show is only a few weeks away. I can't wait to have Koolio out competing — he's so handsome, I bet he'll win lot of ribbons."

"It's not just about looks — the ponies also have to be well trained," Vicki said. "You'll need to teach Koolio a lot before he'll be able to win in the show ring."

"Let's get riding, then," Kelly grinned, tapping her heels against her new pony's sides.

As the sisters walked their ponies to the front paddock, Kelly tried to stay relaxed but Koolio was shifting around uneasily, spooking at everything he passed. He was even scared of the chickens pecking in the dirt for worms.

By the time they reached the paddock, where Mum was waiting for them, Kelly was a mass of nerves.

"He looks like he's being a handful," Mum said with a frown as Koolio darted through the gateway.

"He's pretty scary when he leaps about." In spite of her effort to stay calm Kelly's voice wavered, and her knuckles were white from clutching the reins.

"Just remember that he's barely left his old property before, so everything will be new for him," Mum told her. "I'm sure he'll settle once he's had a good look at everything."

"I hope so," Kelly said, squaring her shoulders in her best attempt at determination. She couldn't help adding, "But until he does, is it all right if we take it slowly?"

∪ ∪ ∪

A week later, Kelly still didn't trust Koolio enough to canter or jump him.

"But he hasn't done anything wrong," Vicki groaned in frustration when Kelly refused, yet again, to try a faster pace.

"You mean apart from him spooking and jig-jogging all the time," Kelly snapped. She was already annoyed and frustrated with herself for letting fear get the better of her — she didn't need Vicki reminding her as well.

"OK, I guess that's true," Vicki said, as she trotted Dandy in a circle. "But at least he hasn't bucked or reared. If you weren't hanging onto the reins so tight, he'd probably relax and stop jig-jogging, too."

"But I'm worried he'll spook and bolt off," Kelly said. In truth, she couldn't stop imagining all the things that could go wrong. "Once he calms down, I'll start trusting him more to try new things — I promise."

But settling seemed to be the last thing on Koolio's mind. After days of slow work, he was full of energy and coiled up like a spring. As Kelly trotted him in the training paddock alongside the river, a pair of ducks suddenly flew up. Koolio bolted forward and, unprepared for the sudden burst of speed, Kelly lost her balance and tumbled to the ground. Spooked by his falling rider, the terrified pony kicked out, his hoof clipping Kelly's shoulder. She cried out in pain, clutching her arm.

The family all came running over, but Vicki was the first to reach her. "Are you all right?"

"He kicked me," Kelly sobbed. She rolled over

and glared at Koolio, who was now standing under the trees, his reins trailing on the ground.

"What happened?" asked Dad.

"Just Koolio being difficult again," Kelly sighed. She wiped her face and gingerly rose to her feet, prodding her aching shoulder. Already she could feel a bruise forming. "Maybe I'm not ready for a pony as big and young as he is. I'm not sure what I was thinking."

"You can't give up on him." Amanda looked at her sister in horror. "When Magic was being naughty, I had to keep trying until finally she behaved. Koolio will get better, too."

"Riding just isn't that fun when I'm constantly worried about getting hurt," Kelly said.

"Would you like me to ride him for a while?" Vicki offered. Kelly looked at her sister for a moment before replying with more determination than she felt.

"Thanks, it's nice of you to offer. But what's the point in getting a new pony if I don't even ride him? I'll feel like I'm giving up if you take over. Even though Koolio scares me, I want to figure out how to fix this by myself."

"Let's get you back on then," Mum said, bringing Koolio over. The gelding was much more relaxed now that the ducks were gone, yet still Kelly eyed him warily. Maybe she should have let Vicki ride him, just this once. If he behaved for Vicki, Kelly would be able to feel more confident straight away.

But then she thought of every other pony she'd had: not once had she trained a pony by herself, or solved any issues that came up. She'd always turned to Vicki for help, and, although it produced a good result at the time, Kelly didn't think it had made her a braver rider in the long run.

Determined that this time, with Koolio, she would manage by herself, she took the reins and Mum boosted her into the saddle. She didn't feel brave, but she would pretend she was as fearless as Vicki. Maybe then she'd actually make some progress with Koolio, without her nerves holding her back.

Tapping her heels against Koolio's sides, Kelly urged him into a walk, then a trot. Soon they were circling the paddock again and again. The longer Koolio worked, the more relaxed he seemed.

Deciding Vicki would try a canter at this stage,

Kelly settled deep in the saddle and urged him on. Leaping playfully, Koolio picked up the pace. Although her heart was pounding, Kelly was careful to keep her hands and legs steady so Koolio wouldn't slow into a trot. Vicki had been right: apart from spooking at the ducks, Koolio hadn't bucked or reared while she'd been riding him. It was only her imagination that was conjuring up all the worst-case scenarios.

After cantering in both directions, Kelly dropped Koolio back to a walk with a huge sigh of relief. Patting the pony's neck, she rode up to her family and leapt to the ground. She'd survived her first canter on Koolio since he'd arrived at their property, and though she was too wracked with nerves to enjoy the ride, it hadn't been as bad as she'd feared. Maybe everything would be OK after all.

Chapter 7
Professional Help

But Kelly's optimism was short-lived. The very next time she went to ride Koolio, all her nerves flooded right back. And she had to keep battling them each and every time she rode him. She couldn't stop worrying. What was he going to do next? Was he going to behave, or would he spook again? Would he throw her off? She could handle a few more bruises, but the fear of breaking a bone paralysed her.

The worst of it was that this constant tension was making riding a chore — Kelly rarely found it fun anymore. With Koolio, nothing was easy like it had been with Cameo. Although he'd been well trained by Mary, and Mum and Vicki tried to help out with advice and encouragement, Kelly felt she lacked the experience and strength to get good results from him. He just didn't seem to listen to her — and in fact, it seemed that with every passing day he was getting worse.

"Nothing works," she groaned in despair at the end of another frustrating ride. She'd had Koolio for two weeks now and there was no way the two of them were ready for competitions. "The way he's going, I'll never trust him enough to start jumping him around courses, let alone compete with him. I'm pulling out of competing this season."

"There's no way that's happening." Mum shook her head. "He is far too good looking and way too talented. We just have to figure out how to get you two working as a team."

"I'm trying as hard as I can," Kelly said. "But I don't think Koolio is trying at all."

Later that evening, after Kelly had done her homework, she settled at the kitchen table to look at the calendar of events. Almost every weekend, from October right through to March, was filled with shows that Vicki had highlighted. The season started with Ribbon Days, then progressed to the more serious A&P Shows. She'd even chosen a few One-Day Events, games days and show-jumping competitions to add a bit of variety.

Kelly frowned as she tried to imagine ever being ready to attend a show on Koolio. But she knew that if she missed the earlier, easier shows, it would be much harder to start competing once they got into the swing of the season.

"What's got you so worried?" Dad asked as he came in to make a cup of coffee.

"I was so excited about the show season starting," Kelly said, her shoulders slumped. "But now that Cameo's gone, and Koolio's not going well, I just can't imagine it happening."

"You've improved so much since he arrived, though. With another couple of weeks under your belt, you'll be away laughing."

Kelly laughed at that. "We might be able to get

to a show, sure, but I doubt we'd win anything. I can barely get him to walk, trot and canter nicely, let alone jump."

"But he looked so good when we tried him," Dad said. "I thought he'd be a champion in the making for sure."

"Me, too." Kelly shrugged miserably. "Maybe I'm ruining him — he's only got worse, not better."

"We can't have that." Dad sipped his drink thoughtfully. "Maybe you just need some lessons."

"Vicki and Mum give me lessons every day," Kelly said. "Trust me — it's not helping."

"No, not from them, from an instructor. Remember how much Vicki and Dandy improved when Leah helped them out?"

Kelly glanced up at her dad hopefully. "Can we afford lessons?"

"We'll make it work somehow." Dad said with a frown. "Mum's got money put aside for the show season, so we might have to use some of that."

"And you really think it'd be worth it?"

"Well, it wouldn't hurt to try. If you only ever do what you're currently doing, you'll only ever achieve what you're currently achieving," Dad said. Kelly smiled. She knew this was one of his favourite sayings — but she also knew he was right.

U U U

A week later Vicki and Kelly saddled up Dandy and Koolio for a joint lesson at a nearby arena. Always keen to learn something new, Vicki had decided to join in with Kelly's session.

But Koolio was even more unsettled than normal in the unfamiliar environment. Kelly sighed in frustration. Glancing over at her sister she noticed that Dandy, who had competed for years, was his normal dependable self.

Listening to the cues from the instructor, Kelly and Vicki began warming up their ponies. They were asked to practise transitions between paces, changing between a walk, trot, canter and halt every few minutes.

"No, Kelly, not like that," the instructor called out after a few minutes. "Come into the middle of the arena and watch Vicki for a minute."

Relieved to have a break, Kelly slowed Koolio

and turned him into the centre of the arena. Silently she watched as the instructor pointed out everything that Vicki was doing well, and in comparison everything Kelly had been doing wrong.

"Now, Kelly, I want you to bring Koolio back out on the circle. Let's try that again," said the instructor briskly.

This time Kelly strived to do everything she'd been told, but no matter how hard she tried, Koolio was too tense and still rushed or threw his head up in the transitions.

By the end of the lesson she was exhausted and near tears — and, even worse, Koolio was dripping in sweat and hadn't improved in the slightest, while in comparison Dandy was supple and relaxed.

"That lesson was amazing," Vicki said, as they drove home. "It's the best Dandy's ever been."

"How did you find it, Kelly?" Mum asked.

"I'm not sure I understood the instructor," Kelly said in a small voice. "I tried to do everything she said, but it didn't seem to make a difference."

"Sometimes it takes a while to start seeing results," Mum said, glancing over to reassure her. "I'm sure next week will go better."

"I don't want to keep doing this," Kelly told her mum through her tears at the end of her third lesson. "The instructor keeps yelling at me, or comparing me to always-perfect Vicki, and I feel like a failure. Koolio's not getting any better, and it's not fun. I always end up crying."

More than anything, she wished Vicki wasn't sharing the lessons with her. It was hard listening to her sister always being praised, especially when the instructor only ever criticised her.

"I don't know what else we can try," Mum sighed. "Maybe you will have to spend a few months gaining your confidence, and not worry so much about getting out to shows."

Kelly nodded glumly. She didn't have much choice. The second Ribbon Day of the season had already come and gone, and she'd had to watch from the sidelines as her sisters won fistfuls of ribbons. Although their new five-horse truck wasn't quite finished, Vicki had been able to take both her ponies along to it since Koolio had been left behind, and she'd won Champion on the Flat with Dandy and Champion Hunter on Casper.

Although Kelly knew both of Vicki's ponies had been challenging at first, and that her sister had had her fair share of struggles training them, it was easy to forget that now. She felt a flare of jealousy as they drove home. For the hundredth time she wished Cameo hadn't been sold, or at the very least that she hadn't chosen Koolio to replace her beloved pony.

He might look like a dream, but he certainly didn't behave like one.

Chapter 8
A Deal is Done

Six weeks after Koolio had joined their family, Vicki finally convinced Kelly to take him out for a trek on the neighbouring farm. Up until then Kelly had been too nervous, and even now she was worried about taking the powerful grey out in such wide open spaces.

"He'll be fine," Vicki assured her, as the two of them set off down the road. "He desperately needs a change of scenery. I bet he's sick of always working in a paddock or on an arena."

Kelly nodded. Vicki was probably right, but her

sister's words didn't help ease her worry. Holding the reins tightly, she followed Dandy along the grass verge that led to the neighbour's farm, then halted while Vicki jumped off to open the gate. As usual, Koolio fidgeted and tugged on the reins.

Through the gate, they took off at a trot, then at the base of the hill they broke into a canter. All was going well until, halfway up, Koolio put his head between his front legs and bucked, moving like a roller coaster beneath her. Grabbing at the reins, Kelly hung on tightly, but she was no match for his power. Again she found herself falling, and it seemed as if the dirt came up to meet her as she slammed into the ground.

For a few seconds Kelly lay winded, then slowly she lifted her head and watched as Koolio galloped up the hill after Dandy, the stirrups flapping wildly. Defeated, and so sore she could barely move, Kelly curled up into a ball, willing the dizziness away.

After what seemed like hours she heard approaching hoof beats. She looked up to see Vicki trotting back towards her on Dandy, leading Koolio.

"Are you OK?" Vicki sounded alarmed as she leapt to the ground.

"Just bruised, I hope." Kelly cringed as she struggled to sit up. "But there's no way I'm riding him back."

"That's OK," Vicki assured her. "I can lead him."

Taking a deep breath, Kelly waited for the pain to pass before slowly standing. Every inch of her body felt battered and bruised.

"In fact, I'm not sure I ever want to ride him again," Kelly whispered, her eyes welling with tears.

Vicki frowned. She reached up to pat Koolio's neck. "I'm sure he'll be fine tomorrow — he's just a bit fresh."

Kelly shook her head adamantly, wincing as the pain shot down her back. "I'm serious. I've been trying for so many weeks and in all that time I haven't had a single ride that was remotely fun. I still don't trust him. As soon as we get home I'm going to ask Mum to advertise him for sale, then I'll start looking for a new pony. Something smaller, older and more experienced. Either that or I give up riding for good."

Vicki gave her sister a thoughtful look, then turned to eye both the ponies whose reins she was holding. Dandy stood quietly, resting a back hoof, but as always Koolio was on edge.

"What about Dandy?" Vicki suggested.

"With the money we get from Koolio, I'd never be able to afford a pony as good as him."

"No, not a pony *like* Dandy," Vicki said. "What about swapping Dandy for Koolio?"

Kelly looked at her sister in disbelief. "You'd actually do that? Swap your Supreme Champion for a problem pony?"

"It's a good trade. In a couple of years I'll be too tall for Dandy anyway. This way you'll get a pony you can compete on straight away, and I'll have a younger, bigger version to train up."

Kelly still couldn't quite trust what she was hearing. "Sounds like a good deal for me," she eventually said, "but not for you. Dandy is worth way more than Koolio."

"Ever since I first saw Koolio, I've been dying to have a ride on him. I'm confident he will be as good as Dandy one day."

"Well, if you're sure about this, let's shake on it, then," Kelly said, holding out her hand. "And no going back on your word if Koolio bucks you off or doesn't turn out as well as you hope."

As they shook hands, both sisters couldn't contain their smiles.

Then Vicki said, "I guess we may as well start now." Handing over Dandy's reins, she swung up onto Koolio's back. Kelly couldn't help but admire her sister's confidence as she trotted the grey gelding up the hill.

Kelly stroked Dandy's neck, still unable to comprehend he was hers. Of all the ponies they'd ever owned, he'd been their most successful — the walls of their tiny bedroom, which all three girls shared, was lined with the hundreds of ribbons he'd won, including countless Champions.

Maybe her dreams of winning a Champion could still come true? The difference was just that it wouldn't be with Koolio, as she had imagined. Kelly found herself smiling as she pictured doing a victory lap on Dandy.

As she watched Koolio making his way back down the hill towards her, Kelly noticed her sister's expression mirrored her own.

It seemed that Vicki was equally happy with the trade they'd just made, yet Kelly still couldn't help feeling she had got the better deal.

U U U

Even though the thought of riding Dandy was tempting, after her fall Kelly felt far too stiff to hop on. So she limped slowly home leading her new pony. Beside her, Vicki sat relaxed on Koolio, her reins loose. When he occasionally spooked or jig-jogged, Vicki shortened her reins to correct him, before softening the contact again. Unlike when she'd ridden him, Kelly noticed he relaxed instantly and came back to a walk.

"I think he likes you," Kelly said as they turned down their driveway.

"The feeling's mutual," Vicki grinned as she bent down to pat his arched neck.

Behind them they heard a car approaching. Kelly glanced over her shoulder, waving when she saw that it was Dad and Amanda, returning from hockey practice in town. Dad slowed the car and Amanda leaned out the window.

"Hey! How come you're riding Koolio?" Amanda asked. Her eyes were wide with curiosity.

Drawing their ponies to a stop, Vicki and Kelly

spoke as one. "We swapped ponies."

"For the day?" Dad asked.

"Nope! Forever," Kelly grinned, reaching up to give Dandy a hug. "I fell off Koolio one too many times, and Vicki offered to trade."

Dad raised his eyebrows. "Well, that's a twist I didn't see coming. What a nice thing to do, Vicki."

A few minutes later, as Kelly struggled to unsaddle Dandy, her father's words came back to her. She knew Vicki had sacrificed a lot to offer her Dandy. Turning to her sister, who was sponging off Koolio, she spoke hesitantly.

"Vicki — if you want to change your mind, I'll understand."

Vicki looked at her, incredulous. "You're kidding, right? After riding Koolio, there's no way I'm changing my mind. He's incredible. I couldn't bear the thought of selling Dandy to another family, but if you have him, I'll still see him every day. Besides, I would never go back on my word."

Chapter 9
Changeover

THE NEXT MORNING Kelly woke up early and made her way outside to see her new pony, feeling stiff from her fall the day before. Even though Dandy had been in their family for years, she'd never actually ridden him — although she had tried once. It was when he had been fresh out of the mountains, just a couple of weeks after he'd been started under saddle for the first time. Dandy had been so startled by Vicki trying to leg Kelly up onto his bare back that he'd spun and kicked Kelly on both knees.

But years had passed since then, and Dandy rarely

did anything wrong now. Although he still had the attitude and presence of a once-wild stallion, he also had the training of a champion show pony.

By the time she reached the paddock, Kelly was surprised to find Vicki already had Koolio caught and was grooming him. She felt a flicker of regret as she eyed the handsome gelding, but it was immediately replaced with a sense of relief that she wouldn't have to ride him again.

With a halter slung over her shoulder, Kelly walked up to Dandy to catch him. But rather than standing to be approached, he snorted at her and took off at a gallop. Surprised, Kelly waited for him to settle, then tried again. But Dandy would have none of it.

"Why won't he let me catch him?" Kelly called out to Vicki.

Even from a distance there was no mistaking Vicki's laugh. "He's testing you. I guess you'll just have to keep trying until you've earned his respect."

Rolling her eyes in exasperation, Kelly went after the fleeing pony once again. For forty minutes Dandy sent her on a merry dance, until finally he walked up and let her halter him.

It wasn't quite the start she'd planned for the day, and Kelly's shoulders were hunched as she led him down the hill to join her sisters.

"That took you long enough," Vicki grinned as she walked over leading Casper. Kelly had taken so long to catch Dandy that Vicki had already finished a short training session on Koolio and had put him back in the paddock to graze. Even Amanda, who had been fast asleep when Kelly had headed out, had her pony caught and ready to ride.

"It was like he was wild again," Kelly groaned. "As soon as I got close he'd spin and bolt away."

"That's what he was like when he was first here," Vicki said. "He hasn't done it in years! But I guess I'm the only one who ever handles or rides him, so it might take him a while to get used to someone new."

"Kelly's hardly new," Amanda said, as she picked out Magic's hooves. "Dandy's known her just as long as he's known you."

"Yes, but she's never worked with him before," Vicki said. "I'm sure he'll adjust, but for the first few weeks don't expect too much."

Kelly could feel her enthusiasm for the trade

dimming. She had got rid of one problem pony, but now his replacement was causing trouble.

"Do you think we'll be ready for the Ribbon Day at the end of the month?"

"I'm sure you will be," Vicki reassured her. "I'm planning to ride Koolio there, too."

"Really?" Kelly said, unable to hide her doubt. From what she'd experienced, Koolio wouldn't be ready to compete for months, if not years.

"Two weeks is a long time," Vicki said. "Besides, he was perfect today."

"I don't believe you," Kelly shook her head. Vicki had to be messing with her.

"It's true," Amanda said as she tightened her pony's girth. "I was watching from the kitchen window while I ate my breakfast. Koolio was really relaxed."

Falling silent, Kelly finished saddling Dandy. Although she was relieved that Koolio and Vicki were going well, it also made her think. Maybe all along *she* had been the reason for his bad behaviour?

Less than half an hour later, all her worries were forgotten. Kelly was in love with Dandy. Although he was a lot more challenging than her old pony Cameo, after riding Koolio he seemed like a breeze. Vicki had promised to teach her exactly how he liked to be ridden, and he was going well. From the moment they'd done their first trot, right through to jumping around a course of 70 centimetres, she hadn't been able to wipe the smile off her face.

"You suit him," Amanda said as she rode over. She'd just jumped Magic around the same course, and they both looked very proud of themselves.

"I feel much safer on him," Kelly admitted, leaning over to hug the fiery chestnut. "There's a few things still to improve, especially the catching, but I also couldn't get him working quite as well as he goes for Vicki."

"Don't be too impatient," Vicki said as she rode up beside them. "Remember what Mum always says?"

"It takes six months to get used to a new pony and two years to get the best from them," Amanda recited, with a roll of her eyes. "But I hope it doesn't take that long with Magic. I'd go crazy!"

"And then we'd all go crazy," Vicki grinned. She dismounted and loosened Casper's girth. "Seriously, Kelly, even though Dandy's done really well with me, you can't expect the same results straight away. It'll take him a while to get used to you, and vice versa."

Although she wished it wasn't the case, Kelly knew her sister was right. None of the ponies they'd had over the years had been perfect when they'd first got them, but with a lot of patience, time and training the girls had been able to realise their ponies' potential.

"Maybe I should miss the next few shows and give myself a little more time to get used to him," Kelly said, warming to the idea. "I have been putting a lot of pressure on myself."

"No, I think it'll be good for you to get a few shows under your belt," Vicki said. "But rather than expecting to win ribbons, why don't you pretend they're just training shows — that way you won't be too upset if things don't go to plan. Even if Koolio's a bit green, I'll take him, too."

At first, Kelly felt heartened by her sister's wise words, but all of a sudden at the back of her mind she had a new niggling worry. Last season Vicki and Dandy had been one of the most successful combinations in the region, and had won Champions at most of the shows. What if Kelly couldn't achieve the same results with the same pony? Would she always be riding in her big sister's shadow?

Chapter 10
Show Time

Two weeks later, as she was sent from the ring, Kelly's worst imaginings had come true. Vicki had been called into the winners' circle on Koolio, yet she and Dandy hadn't even placed.

"I don't know how Vicki does it," she said to the rest of the family, who stood watching at the edge of the ring. "Koolio looks like he's been competing for years."

"He does look amazing," Amanda agreed, then added: "Nothing like our scruffy ponies."

"What do you mean?"

"Well, look how dull their coats are, for starters. No one would ever guess that Dandy's a champion show pony from how he looks at the moment."

Kelly glared at her sister, thoroughly insulted. "It's not my fault he likes to roll around in the dirt all the time!"

Mum intervened, holding up a hand to silence them before an argument developed. "Amanda has a good point. Vicki spent hours and hours pulling Koolio's mane and trimming his tail, legs, chin and ears. Then she washed him about five times until he was snow white, and got up at dawn to plait him. She deserves to win after the effort she's put into his presentation and training."

Kelly looked down at Dandy with a newly critical eye. His mane was far too long and thick to plait so she hadn't bothered, nor had she trimmed his tail, which was almost dragging along the ground. Even the hairs under his chin were long and spiky, masking how pretty his head truly was.

Kelly's face reddened. "I guess I kept thinking of this as a training day, so I didn't put in much effort." Hoping to deflect attention away from herself, she turned to Amanda. "What's your excuse?"

"I'm eight years old," her sister replied cheekily, as if that explained everything. "And anyway, it all sounds like too much work. I'll wait till the jumping classes to win some ribbons — it doesn't matter what the ponies look like in those classes."

∪ ∪ ∪

By lunchtime, once all the flat classes were complete, Kelly and Amanda had won only one ribbon each — both in their rider class, which was judged on how well the girls had ridden, as opposed to how well the ponies looked or performed. By contrast, Vicki and Koolio had placed in all seven classes they'd entered. Several times, as Kelly watched Koolio gracefully circling the judge, she wondered if perhaps she'd given up on him too soon. Maybe if she'd been a little bit braver, it would be her out there winning handfuls of ribbons, rather than her sister. Koolio was by far the classiest horse at the Ribbon Day, and she couldn't help being filled with a sense of regret.

But while the flat classes proved to be Koolio's

strength, the jumping soon showcased his weakness. After several refusals, Vicki managed to get him over every jump, but even then he was hesitant and leapt awkwardly over many of the fences. Dandy and Magic, on the other hand, jumped around like seasoned competitors and raked in the ribbons.

Kelly's spirits were much higher as she piloted Dandy around the challenging Handy Hunter course. Approaching the jumps at nice sharp angles, they flew around the course, and Kelly felt as if they were flying. Dandy was far more nimble than Cameo had ever been, and as she dropped him back to a walk she couldn't hide her delight.

Soon it was her little sister's turn, and Kelly watched as Amanda and Magic jumped quietly around the course. The two of them did well together, although Amanda took the turns much wider, which would result in a lower score. Vicki and Koolio were the last to go, and again the young pony struggled to jump around clear. Now it was Vicki leaving the ring with no ribbons, while Kelly was called forward to take the top prize. Amanda finished in fourth place.

Anxious that Vicki would be upset about how

badly Koolio was jumping, Kelly rode straight out of the ring after her lap of honour and approached her sister. "You're not regretting swapping, are you?" Kelly asked Vicki, her face creased in worry.

But to her surprise Vicki didn't seem upset in the slightest. In fact, she looked startled. "Why would I be? Koolio cleaned up this morning."

"He doesn't seem to be very good at jumping, though," Kelly said cautiously.

"You're kidding, right? He's probably the best jumping pony I've ever sat on. He's going to be a superstar."

Kelly was dumbfounded. "But he's had at least one refusal in every round, and he's spooking at everything."

Vicki's grin widened. "But occasionally, when he gets everything right, his jumps are huge over the fences. He's allowed to be green and wobbly today. I'm planning ahead to how he'll be performing six months from now. And, trust me, this pony's going to be a star."

"I really hope you're right," Kelly said, but she was still laced with doubt. While she might have wished she'd still owned Koolio after watching him win in the morning, after watching him jump, Kelly was pleased her sister had taken him over. Even with Vicki's added strength, he'd still looked like a handful.

Chapter 11
Unwanted Advice

BY THE END OF THEIR FIRST SHOW, Kelly and Dandy had added a colourful array of ribbons to the family's collection. She couldn't wait for their next competition, but first Dandy was in desperate need of a makeover. Kelly felt terrible for sabotaging his chances at the show's first classes by turning him out so poorly.

For the next few days, Kelly and Amanda spent hours grooming their ponies. With every stroke of the curry comb, their coats began to gleam and soon the chestnut and bay shone like copper pennies.

Now Dandy no longer looked like he'd come straight out of the mountains, Kelly focused on tidying up the last of his scruffy hairs. She trimmed his tail to just the right length, then Vicki helped her clip the hair from his legs and chin.

"That's the Dandy I remember," Vicki said fondly, as she stood back to admire their handiwork. "It was hard to recognise him under all that fluff."

"I still can't believe we took Magic and Dandy to the Ribbon Day looking so unloved." Amanda hung her head in embarrassment.

"Well, we won't make the same mistake again," Kelly said firmly. "We might have got away with it at a Pony Club Ribbon Day, but it's only a month until our first A&P Show and there's no way we'd survive the disgrace if we turned up looking like that."

"We'd be laughed out of the ring," Amanda giggled. Kelly quickly joined in, imagining all the posh riders turning up their noses at them.

"You probably need to school them a little better before then as well," Vicki said, cutting through her sisters' laughter.

Falling silent, Kelly looked at Vicki in surprise. "You told me I was going really well on Dandy."

"You are," Vicki assured her, "considering you've only had him for a month. But he's capable of doing much better. You need to learn how to ride Dandy properly if you want to win a Champion like you've always dreamed of."

"So you're saying you ride him better than I do?" But even as she said it, Kelly knew it was a silly question. Not only was Vicki two years older than her, and with much more riding experience, she also had an innate talent with horses that was undeniable.

"Not necessarily better," Vicki said diplomatically. "But after riding Dandy for the past few years, I do know how he likes to be ridden."

For the next week Kelly continued riding Dandy the same way she always did. Twice she cantered around the farm, which was her favourite way of passing time in the saddle, and twice she rode him in the paddock. During these sessions, however, her attention span was short. Schooling her ponies was something she'd never really enjoyed, and after even a few minutes of riding in a circle she grew bored, and went off to trot up and down hills and canter over ditches.

Her second Ribbon Day on Dandy was coming up the following weekend and Kelly spent the day before washing him and cleaning her gear. She even braided Dandy's recently pulled mane. Although she hadn't invested much time into his training, he certainly looked the part, and she was confident they'd do much better and win more ribbons.

∪ ∪ ∪

But the next day, as they drove home after the show, she began to wonder if Vicki had been right. Again, Kelly and Dandy had won ribbons only in the rider and hunter classes. In the flat classes, in which Dandy normally excelled, the judges had barely looked at him. Not once had she and Dandy even made it into the top six, who got to do individual workouts before the judges chose the placegetters.

"What am I doing wrong?" Kelly asked her sister. "I made sure that Dandy looked a million dollars, but the judge still chose plainer horses over us."

"You really want to know?" Vicki said.

Nodding, Kelly waited impatiently for her sister's reply.

"When he's in the ring, he looks like he's barely trained."

"He would have won more Champions than any other pony at the show!" Kelly broke into a fit of laughter. "And at events far more prestigious than Ribbon Days."

"But you'd never guess that by looking at him now," Vicki said frankly. "He's not soft and supple, or working in the correct frame."

Kelly felt like the wind had been knocked out of her. She realised the truth of her sister's words, but she couldn't help the anger that flared inside her.

"It's not my fault you didn't train him properly," she snapped.

"We won Supreme Champion in the last show I rode him at," Vicki retorted. "He was judged the very best — from all the ponies at the show, across every ring. So don't you tell me I didn't train him properly. You're the one who's not riding him well enough."

"Girls!" Dad said firmly. "That's enough."

Kelly glared at her big sister. She was fuming. Yet there was no denying that she could see a pattern forming. Koolio had performed terribly for her, and now, with Vicki, he was consistently winning. Dandy, who'd previously won everything with Vicki, wasn't placing in any of the flat classes now Kelly was riding him. And yet surely her riding couldn't be at fault when she almost always won her rider classes, both on the flat and over hurdles?

"It doesn't make sense," Kelly said after a long silence. "The judges obviously think I'm a good rider."

"You're a pretty rider," Mum said hesitantly, "but not always the most effective."

Kelly's anger flared again, and she struggled to keep her voice even. "What do you mean 'not effective'?"

"At home you mostly ride for fun," Mum said kindly. "You don't put the hours into the ponies' training like Vicki does, and you don't have the same expectations of them to work correctly. Most of the time, even at shows, you ride around on a long rein and your ponies don't work on the bit, which is what the judges expect."

"Vicki takes her ponies on farm rides all the time, too," Kelly grumbled.

"Yes, she does," Mum said. "But a couple of times a week she schools them in the paddock, too, and not just riding around like hooligans like you and Amanda. Don't get me wrong — there's nothing wrong with that, if you lower your expectations and don't expect to win in the classes that require a well-trained pony."

"But I do want to win the flat classes."

"Then take your sister's advice, let her give you some lessons, and let's see if you can get Dandy going as well as he's capable of."

"I can't have lessons with Vicki at the moment." Kelly's voice shook. "She'll just make me mad."

"What about that riding instructor we were using with Koolio?" Dad suggested.

Kelly shook her head. "No way! I always end up in tears when she's teaching me."

"It might be different with Dandy," Mum said, but Kelly was not to be moved.

"If we can find someone to teach me who doesn't make me either sad or mad, we can try again,"

Kelly declared, her voice wobbly. "But until then, maybe I'll just give up on my dreams of winning a Champion."

Chapter 12
A Close Call

VICKI AND KELLY BARELY SPOKE for two days following their argument. But on Tuesday morning, as Kelly was packing her school lunchbox, Vicki burst into the house.

"Koolio's missing!" she cried, her eyes wide with fear.

"Everyone — outside now!" Dad ordered. "No one's going to school until he's found."

Immediately forgetting her differences with her sister, Kelly rushed outside.

Splitting into groups, the family first scoured

every inch of their own property, before heading up the road, checking in back yards and on the grass reserves, keeping an eye out for the missing pony. They even stopped passing cars and knocked on doors.

"Excuse me, but you haven't seen a grey pony, by any chance?" Vicki asked as the door of a small townhouse was opened by a black-haired woman wearing jeans and a polo shirt.

"No, I haven't," the lady replied. "You're one of the girls from down the hill, right? I often see you riding past with your sisters."

"That's them," Mum said from the base of the steps to the front door. "Vicki's pony went missing overnight."

"Do you want a hand searching for him?" the lady said, stepping out the door and pulling on some riding boots.

"We didn't know that you're a horsey person!" Vicki exclaimed.

"My name's Sarah, and I've ridden my whole life," she replied. "Now, where haven't you searched?"

An hour later they'd looked everywhere within a kilometre radius of their property, with no luck. They'd even phoned the local police to see if anyone had reported seeing a lost pony, but they'd heard nothing.

They stood in a circle in the driveway, talking over what to do next.

"What if he's been stolen?" Kelly said, voicing her greatest fear.

"He has to be somewhere," Dad said, his forehead creased in worry. "I'll head out in the car and search further afield."

"I'll run home and get my car, too," Sarah offered.

"Good idea," Dad said. "We'll halve the time if two of us search."

"What about the rest of us?" Vicki said. "It'll drive us crazy if we stay behind doing nothing."

"Mum can stay here, just in case the police call. Kelly and Amanda, you go with Sarah and keep a look-out while she's driving, and Vicki, you come with me."

But just as they were about to head off, Dad froze. "You did check the river when you searched his paddock, right?"

Unease filled Kelly as she watched Vicki's face go stark white. Then suddenly Vicki turned, sprinting away in the direction of the river paddocks. Forgetting their plans, everyone followed her, their movements clumsy in their haste. Jumping over the fence, Kelly struggled to keep up with the adults' longer legs. She was out of breath by the time they reached the deep river that flowed along the boundary of the 2.5 hectare reserve the Wilsons leased from the council. Spreading out, everyone began looking for skid marks on the steep banks that lined the water's edge.

"The water's murky," Dad said, pointing, his voice grim. "Something upstream has stirred up mud from the river floor."

He took off upstream at a run, his pace relentless as he weaved between trees and jumped over fences, his eyes scouring the river.

"Koolio!" Kelly called out, as terror filled her, and she ran after Dad at top speed.

"He's here! I've found him," Vicki's choked cry

filled the air. Kelly followed her dad as he changed his course, taking the most direct route towards where they'd heard Vicki's voice.

"Is he OK?" Dad called when she was finally within sight.

"His head's only just above the water," Vicki replied in a panic. "And he's shaking so hard."

Skidding to a stop beside her, Kelly and Dad looked in horror at the largely submerged pony, who stood completely still in the water, only his terrified eyes flicking in their direction.

"The water's well over his back — we're lucky he hasn't drowned. Another hour and he probably would have been too exhausted to keep his head above water."

"How on earth will we get him out?" Kelly asked as she took in the steep river banks, which dropped a metre down to the water below.

"We'll need a halter and lots of ropes," Dad told Mum, Sarah and Amanda, who'd just rushed up to join them at the river bank. Kelly rushed back to the tack shed to help them. Standing there watching Koolio as he struggled to keep his head above the water was almost unbearable. She was only too willing to put distance between herself and the very

real life-or-death situation.

"Hurry!" Vicki called out as they raced back with the gear.

Dad outlined his rescue plan.

"Vicki, you're going to jump in and swim slowly over to him, so as not to scare him, and get a halter on him. Then we're going to have to tie long ropes to either side of his halter and lead him up the river. We'll have one person on each river bank holding the ropes, to keep him swimming straight. About a hundred metres upstream the bank's not quite as steep, and we might be able to get him out."

Kelly watched as her dad carefully lowered Vicki down into the chilly water so she didn't jump in and make a big splash. But even then Koolio snorted and tried to move, stirring up fresh mud as he panicked in the deep water.

"Give him a second," Dad instructed, his voice tight.

Pausing, Vicki treaded water until Koolio regained his footing, his head dropping even lower in the water until only his eyes, ears and nostrils were visible. Vicki slowly edged closer, her heart pounding as Koolio's gaze never left hers, the whites of his eyes showing in panic.

"You're OK, boy," Vicki whispered, as she reached out and drew the halter over his muzzle. Kelly caught her breath as Vicki fought to buckle the halter, her fingers fumbling beneath the dark water.

"It's done." Relief filled Vicki's voice as she swam over to the river bank to catch the ropes being passed down to her. Then she swam back to Koolio, clipping on a lead before swimming back to the edge and passing it up to Dad. She then repeated the process, this time taking a rope to Mum, who was now standing on the far bank, dripping wet after swimming across the river.

In spite of all the commotion, Koolio didn't move a muscle. Even when they tightened the ropes and tried to pull him up the river he didn't budge.

"He's given up," Kelly cried as Koolio sank even lower in the water, precariously close to sinking beneath the surface completely.

"His cover will be weighing him down," Mum called out to Vicki. "See if you can undo it and drag it off him."

Kelly's heart was in her mouth as she watched Vicki dive under the water to undo the cover straps.

Finally, she emerged, gasping for breath, before ducking back under.

"There's eight straps," Amanda whispered as she reached out and clutched Kelly's hand. For what seemed like an eternity they waited for Vicki to resurface each time, her arms flailing in exhaustion and her teeth chattering as she attempted to tug off the sodden cover. Finally, Vicki managed to pull it away completely. She let it go and swam for the bank, the cover brushing past Koolio's sides as it floated away downstream.

Startled by the movement of the cover, and with the extra weight gone from his body, Koolio suddenly came to life. He reared up in the water, before leaping forward. Her hands clutched together in fright, Kelly watched as her parents kept his momentum going with their ropes, the exhausted grey battling for his life. Finally they reached a point where he could stumble up the muddy incline and onto high ground. Then his trembling legs collapsed and he dropped to the ground.

Chapter 13
Practice Makes Perfect

While Koolio recovered from his river ordeal, Sarah, their neighbour from up the road, visited often to check up on him. She'd only just moved into the area and seemed to be enjoying spending free time with the Wilsons and their animals.

Not only had Koolio been exhausted and at risk of catching a chill, but branches beneath the river's surface had left several cuts on his legs. Although none of the injuries were serious, it took a couple of weeks for him to return to full health.

Sarah was more than happy to help poultice and

bandage Koolio's wounds and Vicki was happy to have her company. She, Kelly and Amanda spent hours talking with Sarah while they tended Koolio, and were intrigued to learn that she was an A&P Show judge. Not only that, but she also had a long list of national titles to her name from years of competing in the show ring. With no horses of her own at the moment, she was only too happy to help them with their ponies, and they all benefited from her expertise.

"That's perfect," Sarah exclaimed, as Kelly and Dandy completed a mock workout she'd designed for the three of them. For the last two weeks she'd been giving Kelly lessons, and as her style was to encourage Kelly rather than criticise her, Kelly worked hard and the improvement was obvious. "I think you're ready for this weekend."

Anticipation, rather than anxiety, filled Kelly at the thought of competing at her first A&P Show on Dandy. Not only were they working together better than ever, but she was getting a huge feeling of satisfaction each time she mastered a new skill.

"Thanks for teaching me," Kelly said, as she lined Dandy up beside her sisters and their ponies.

"I've learnt so much from you."

"You're welcome," Sarah smiled, as she motioned for Amanda to begin her workout. "It's been fun watching how far you've progressed."

"He's looking amazing," Vicki whispered to Kelly from where she sat on Koolio. The grey had fully recovered from his river ordeal and was back to full fitness. "Better than amazing, actually."

As Kelly sat lightly in the saddle, she realised how much she'd been enjoying the schooling sessions on Dandy. She used to think training her pony on the flat was a chore, but now, for the first time, she could see the benefit of it — and she loved the results she was getting. It would be interesting to see if the extra training made any difference to their performance in the show ring, but Kelly didn't want to let her hopes get too high, for fear of being disappointed.

The last thing they needed to do before the A&P Show was to put the finishing touches on their new horse truck. The ramp was on, a bench had been built, rubber matting had been laid on the floor, and dividers installed to separate the horses while they travelled. There were even five beds, a kitchen sink and a shower so they could sleep overnight in the truck at shows, saddle and bridle racks to keep their tack tidy, cupboards and drawers for their clothes, and a locker for hay.

"Now it just needs a paint job," Dad said on Wednesday afternoon as he finished chaining up the last bunk, which hung from the roof so it could be folded up when it wasn't in use. "But I'll leave that to you girls — my work is done."

"What colour shall we choose?" Mum said, running her hands over the thick plywood which lined the walls.

"Blue," all three girls said at the same time.

"Blue it is," Mum grinned. "I'm running out of time to get everything done by myself. I'll ring up the school tomorrow and let them know you'll be staying home to help me all day. We'll head into town first thing in the morning to pick up some cans of paint, and some foam to make mattresses for the beds. Then we can spend all day working on the truck."

By eleven the next morning, the back of the horse truck was filled with their purchases. The girls tied their hair back and put on old clothes in case they got paint on themselves.

First, they painted everything with a white undercoat paint. While they waited for this coat to dry they used chalk to trace bed-shapes on the foam, then Mum used a sharp knife to cut the mattresses to size.

Next Mum showed Kelly how to measure up and sew fabric to cover the foam, so the mattresses would stay clean. The fabric was blue to match the paint.

While Mum and Kelly sewed, Vicki and Amanda unpacked their old truck and washed it down, so it would be ready to sell. Both were huge jobs, and by the time they were complete the first coat of paint was dry.

"Vicki and Kelly, you paint all the walls pale blue," Mum said as she poured paint into a tray and handed them each a roller. "Amanda, you're with me. We'll paint the bench navy."

Soon the entire interior was painted in different shades of blue. Kelly couldn't help but admire their handiwork. "I can't wait until the paint's dry so we

can put the mattresses in place and start packing all our gear into it."

"That can be tomorrow afternoon's job." Mum smiled as she rinsed out the paint brushes and rollers. "I'll do the final coat in the morning while you're at school, so it has plenty of time to dry."

"Can't we miss another day to help out?" Amanda begged.

"Please — I learned way more today than I would

have in class," Kelly added, thinking about all the sewing they'd done.

Mum hesitated, then nodded. "It would help me a lot. I'll give the school a ring and see if they'd mind", she conceded. "We can paint the old truck, too, so it looks a little tidier before we take photos to advertise it."

U U U

Late the next afternoon, Kelly and her sisters hung the last of their showing outfits in the truck's cupboard. It had taken them hours to transfer everything into the new truck, but, even with the beds made up, everything seemed much roomier than what they were used to. The only thing missing was their saddlery, which they'd clean and pack after they'd ridden their ponies on Saturday.

"There's so much space!" Kelly said, waving her arms in delight. "It's so nice having a place to put everything."

"We'll need the extra room, now that we'll have to pack gear for four ponies instead of three," Amanda said. Their last truck had only had a narrow locker to put their gear in, and often they'd had to pile things on the floor, or on their laps in the cab, because there wasn't enough space.

"Dinner's almost ready," Dad called out, knocking on the truck door. "Am I allowed to look yet?" From the moment they'd begun painting the day before, he had been banished from checking in to see how the truck was progressing.

"We've just finished," Amanda said as she opened the door, letting him in. "What do you think?"

His eyes widened when he saw what they'd achieved. "It's very blue," he said, as his eyes roved from the navy benches to the pale blue walls.

"I can't believe we got it finished in time. I was worried we'd have to take the smaller truck instead and I'd have to leave Casper behind this weekend," Vicki said.

"We really did leave it till the last minute, didn't we?" Dad said as he opened the drawers and saw they'd been stacked with the mismatched plates and cups they'd picked up at a garage sale.

"We colour-coordinated as much as possible," Kelly said proudly.

"It looks great, but there's just one thing missing."

Kelly frowned, glancing around to see what they'd forgotten.

"Tomorrow we'll have to get Mum to paint some horses along the beam on the edge of the beds," Dad said decisively. "That'd make it perfect."

"Oh, yes!" Kelly grinned. Their mum was a brilliant artist and used to have her paintings in galleries before she'd gotten too busy running around after Kelly and her sisters to find the time to paint. Like her mum, Kelly also had a gift for painting and she had even had one of her paintings included in an exhibition. "Maybe she'll let me help?"

"I'm sure she will," Dad said. "It sure is good having two artists in the family."

Chapter 14
Almost a Champion

SATURDAY WAS CHAOTIC as they got everything ready for their first A&P Show of the season. The most time-consuming task was getting Casper's and Koolio's coats back to white, as they were stained yellow from rolling in clay. As soon as Magic and Dandy were clean, Amanda and Kelly pitched in to help, soaping and scrubbing Vicki's ponies' legs and tails until mud no longer ran off them.

"How did I end up with two grey ponies anyway?" Vicki moaned an hour later, when she noticed Koolio had rolled again in his yard.

"Because of your generous nature," Kelly laughed, eyeing the filthy pony, who now looked more brown than grey. "That's yet another reason I'm so glad you traded ponies. Chestnuts are so much easier to keep clean!"

"Then you can help me wash him again," Vicki grumbled, as she caught Koolio and led him over to the hose.

This time Vicki was careful to keep Koolio tied up, with a slice of hay, until he was dry. While they waited, they sat on the ramp of the truck cleaning their gear, making the most of the afternoon sunshine.

"That's everything done," Amanda grinned, as she placed her well-oiled saddle carefully on the rack.

"No, it's not," Kelly said, jumping up and running down the ramp. "We forgot to paint the horses!"

A few minutes later, she returned with Mum in tow. Mum carefully painted a row of white horses walking, trotting and cantering along the length of the beam, while Kelly used the navy paint to shade them. Dad arrived just as she was painting the mane and tail on the final horse.

"Good team effort," Mum said, giving everyone a high-five. "I never imagined our new truck would look this good!"

"It's not about how good the truck looks, it's about how good the ponies inside it are — right, girls?" their dad said.

"We do have some pretty nice ponies," Vicki said, smiling.

"That's all because of you girls," Mum said, her voice proud. "Not many riders could have turned ponies that cost so little into champions."

"They're not all champions yet," Kelly pointed out as she eyed Koolio, who now grazed peacefully in his paddock.

"Don't doubt him for a second," Vicki said confidently. "The judges will love Koolio."

∪ ∪ ∪

"They're waiting for you at the ring," Vicki said the next day as she cantered up on Koolio, a red ribbon fluttering from his neck. Just like she'd predicted, the judge had been smitten by the gorgeous grey, and he'd won all his novice classes.

"The Junior Ring has stopped for a lunch break," Kelly said as she finished unbraiding Dandy's mane before the hunter classes began that afternoon. She and Amanda had completed their flat classes much earlier than their older sister. Now that Vicki was thirteen, she had moved up to the Intermediate Ring and they no longer competed against her.

"Didn't you hear them calling you for the judging of Junior Champion on the Flat?" Vicki said.

"But I didn't win my Open Pony class," Kelly said, confused. She was sure that she would have had to win Dandy's height class to qualify for Champion.

"No, but you won Best Paced and Mannered, right? You better saddle up fast."

"Right!" Kelly gasped, as she glanced at her unsaddled and unbraided pony in shock. She'd always dreamed of being eligible to compete for a Champion, but now that she had the chance there was no way she'd be able to get Dandy ready in time.

"I'll ride back and tell them you're coming — you've got about two minutes!" Vicki said.

Mum and Dad quickly helped Kelly saddle and bridle Dandy. "There's nothing we can do about the plaits, but hopefully the judge can look past that," Mum soothed.

Feeling flustered, Kelly cantered over to the ring, weaving between dozens of horse trucks. Three other riders were already there.

Kelly slotted Dandy into place between the other ponies, struggling to catch her breath. But in spite of their mad dash to the ring, Dandy seemed to understand how important the occasion was and performed better than ever as the judge put them through their paces.

"Good boy," Kelly whispered, as the judge called all the riders into the centre of the ring, lining the ponies up head to tail to compare their looks and conformation. Although each pony's training was important, choosing a Champion was just as much a beauty contest, and Kelly knew it. She just hoped they wouldn't be marked down too much for Dandy's mane not being plaited.

Kelly felt filled with butterflies as she waited for the judges' decision. She had no doubt that she and Dandy had never performed better. No matter their final placing, she was so proud of how far they'd come.

"Can I please have Just Fine 'n' Dandy as Reserve Champion," the judge called out.

Kelly let out a gasp as she rode Dandy forward to receive his lilac sash, the first she'd ever won. She could hardly believe she'd won Reserve at her first A&P Show on Dandy. Glancing over to where Vicki sat astride Koolio clapping in congratulations, she flashed her sister a wide, grateful smile, knowing that without her it would never have been possible.

υ υ υ

Three hours later, Kelly and her sisters lined up at the main oval, their ponies' necks decorated with ribbons of every colour. Six Champions took the lead: there was a Champion on the Flat and a Champion Hunter from each of the Junior, Intermediate and Senior rings. Among them were Vicki on Casper, who'd won Champion Hunter for his third time. To Kelly's delight, Vicki had also won Reserve Champion on the Flat on Koolio. Not wanting either pony to miss out on the Grand Parade, Vicki had Koolio on the lead behind Casper.

Next in line were the Reserve Champions, and Kelly proudly took her place. Dandy arched his neck as the procession began, showing off his lilac sash, as well as two red and three blue ribbons. It was, without a doubt, Kelly's most successful A&P Show. As they circled the oval, followed by a hundred other horses and ponies, she took a snapshot in her mind so she wouldn't forget the moment.

As the Grand Parade came to an end, Kelly spied Sarah waiting beside their parents. She'd been judging the Senior Ring all day, and Kelly couldn't wait to show her all the ribbons she'd won. Trotting over, she untied Dandy's Reserve sash and waved it for her to see.

"What did you win?" Sarah asked as they drew closer. A flicker of recognition danced across her face as she eyed Dandy's mane, which was still curly from his plaits.

"Wait, let me guess." Sarah held up a hand, bursting into a fit of laughter. "You were the girl who won Reserve Champion on the Flat in the Junior Ring, aren't you?"

Kelly nodded, unsure what was so funny.

"The judge was telling us the story at lunchtime,"

she said, her face sympathetic. "He'd planned to give you Champion, but then you showed up unplaited."

"Really?" Kelly gasped, her eyes wide with wonder. "He thought we were good enough to win Champion?"

Sarah nodded. "Next time, keep those plaits in. You'll be leading a Grand Parade before you know it."

As Kelly rode back to the truck, she was kicking herself for not checking whether she'd qualified for Champion before she'd taken a lunch break. She wouldn't make that mistake again.

Chapter 15
Where There's a Will, There's a Way

WITH A MONTH BEFORE the next A&P Show, Kelly and her sisters attended Pony Club every Wednesday evening after school. On weekends they tried out a number of different competitions: show jumping, a One-Day Event, and representing their Pony Club at Zone Games, the regional Games championships.

"I've never seen such versatile ponies." Sarah shook her head in disbelief as they filled her in on some of their latest adventures. "Most show riders would never dream of taking their horses outside of an arena, let alone do half the things you three get up to!"

"Really?" Amanda said in surprise. "If I had to ride around in circles all the time I'd probably die of boredom!"

"I know a lot of riders who are too scared to ride in large open spaces," Sarah said. "They'd have a panic attack even going out on a farm ride with you girls."

"And I thought *I* was nervous on horseback," Kelly said.

"Maybe in comparison to your sisters," Sarah laughed. "But compared to most riders, you're brave."

Kelly rolled her eyes. "I still have plenty of fears."

"Then that makes you twice as courageous," Sarah said with conviction. "Courage is not a lack of fear, but being able to face the things that scare you and do them anyway."

"But Koolio scared me and I gave up on him," Kelly countered. "I still feel bad about that."

"If I hadn't offered you Dandy in a weak moment, I doubt you would've given up on him," Vicki spoke up. "You were just frustrated and sore at the time."

"Maybe that's true," Kelly conceded, after a few

moments mulling it over. "Although I couldn't be happier about how things turned out."

"In that case, I'll stop feeling bad that I took advantage of you in a weak moment," Vicki said. "Koolio's the most talented pony I've ever sat on."

Sarah nodded. "I've been judging for over a decade and he's one of the best ponies I've ever seen, too."

"What about Dandy?" Kelly demanded in mock outrage.

"And Magic!" Amanda cut in.

"They're both doing well at the local shows," Sarah reassured them. "But Koolio's in a whole other league. He could win at national level."

"You really think so?" asked Vicki breathlessly.

"I know so," Sarah said. "If you want to compete in the open classes at the Royal Show, I'll help you train for it. I'll even come with you as your groom to help prepare your ponies."

"When is it?" Kelly asked, excited by the prospect of her sister competing against the best riders in the country.

"Less than two months away." Sarah frowned. "We'd have our work cut out for us, but I think we could get you all ready in time."

"All of us?" Amanda said in shock. "I thought you said only Koolio was good enough."

"On the flat, for sure," Sarah said. "But you and Kelly are some of the best riders I've seen for your age. You both should enter your rider championships and the hunter classes."

"Are you sure we shouldn't wait until next year?" Vicki sounded doubtful. "Koolio's only done a handful of shows and he's still pretty inexperienced."

"And we don't have the right gear, either," Kelly sighed. "We've done our best, but we still look like country bumpkins in comparison to some of the proper show riders. It didn't matter so much when we competed in the novice classes, but in the open classes we'll stand out like sore thumbs."

"Don't let that stop you for a second," Sarah said firmly. "Trust me, I know all the tricks to get both you and your ponies up to standard."

"So let's say we did decide to compete at the Royal Show — what would we need to do?" Vicki asked, unable to contain her curiosity.

"First, get your parents on board, then we can make a plan."

Two days later, after considering all the costs of entering the Royal Show, and the distance they'd have to drive, their parents finally reached a decision.

"The suspense is killing me," Kelly groaned as their parents sat them down to talk after they got home from school.

"We just don't have the funds for that type of show at the moment," Dad began, his expression apologetic. "It would cost over five hundred dollars for the entry fees and diesel alone, and unfortunately the new horse truck and the lessons have used up the last of our savings."

Dead silence followed his announcement. Kelly's shoulders slumped as she glanced at her sisters.

"But," Mum continued, "the answer's not *no*, but rather: *how* can we make it happen? I've called the local high school and they might be able to give me a few hours' relief teaching, but we've only got three weeks until the entries close and it won't bring in anywhere near enough money."

"Wait two seconds," Kelly said, holding up her hand before dashing from the room. The situation felt uncannily like when they were trying to raise enough funds to save Casper, and it reminded her of ways they'd found enough money back then.

Returning with their three piggy-banks, she passed her sisters' ones to them. Together they emptied their contents into three separate piles, counting how much they'd managed to save.

"I've got forty-two dollars," Amanda piped up.

"Seventy-four," Vicki said a few moments later.

Kelly's eyes widened in shock as she finished counting her own. Surely that couldn't be right? She pushed her pile of coins and notes towards her dad. "Can you double-check for me?"

"Two hundred and thirty-nine dollars," Dad said as he quickly counted again. "What did you get?"

"The same!" Kelly laughed in disbelief — it was the most money she'd ever had in her life. "I haven't checked in over a year, but I've made and sold quite a few show browbands and rope halters since then."

"That's almost enough," Mum said, looking between her daughters. "It's mostly your money, though, Kelly, so I guess it's up to you. You might get some back if any of you win prize money, but there's no guarantees."

Glancing at her sisters' hopeful expressions, Kelly shrugged, then let out a massive whoop.

"We're going to the Royal Show!"

Watching Vicki's jaw drop in gratitude and delight, Kelly decided it was worth every cent.

"Can we run up to Sarah's and tell her?" Amanda begged, already heading for the door.

"Sure, but make sure you're back in time for dinner!" Mum said. Her reply was lost as Vicki and Kelly sprinted after their little sister, the door slamming behind them.

Chapter 16
Dressed to Kill

"So WHAT'S THE FIRST THING we need to work on?" Vicki asked after they had babbled out their good news to Sarah.

"Follow me," Sarah said.

They all quickly complied, eager to see what Sarah had to show them. Walking down to the end of the hallway, they entered a room that was lined from ceiling to floor with horse gear, photographs and hundreds of ribbons.

"I wasn't expecting a tack room in the middle of your townhouse!" Amanda giggled.

"Even though I haven't competed for years, I couldn't bear to part with any of it. Everything in here brings back such good memories," Sarah said.

Pointing out different bridles and saddles, as well as an assortment of other gear, Sarah told them what she'd won using the gear, and which horse she'd been riding.

"This is the saddle I used when I won the Sue Yearbury Memorial," she said as she ran her hand over a stunning show saddle. Not a single piece of metal was showing; even the domes were covered in leather.

"Where did you win this wreath?" Kelly asked, as her hands hovered over an exquisite ring of red roses.

"I won that on Ace of Diamonds at the Premier Championships." Sarah smiled as the memory came back to her. She lifted up a silver plate and a blood-red ribbon, etched with gold writing. "This is the trophy and sash that match the garland."

Vicki looked reverently at the prizes. "I've never seen anything like this in my life."

"Me neither," Kelly whispered in awe as she gazed around the room.

"It certainly makes me miss my riding days," Sarah said wistfully. "Judging just isn't the same. But I'm quite enjoying helping you three with your ponies!"

"But after seeing all this, there's no way we can compete at the Royal Show," Vicki said. "I'd fooled myself into thinking it was possible, but never in a million years could we ever afford this type of gear."

"But that's the beauty of it," Sarah said, as she began pulling gear off the racks. "You don't need to. You can borrow all of mine."

"You can't be serious!" Vicki shook her head. "It must be worth thousands."

"Unfortunately, most of it will be too big for Dandy or Magic, but Koolio will fit everything." Sarah sized up the three girls. "Some of my riding clothes might even fit you, too, Vicki, although I think they would swamp Kelly and Amanda."

Kelly's eyes boggled as Sarah threw open the wardrobe and started shuffling through a collection of outfits. There were black, navy, grey and brown riding jackets, and riding shirts and ties in every colour of the rainbow.

"What's this for?" Kelly asked, pointing to a

woollen waistcoat with a silk handkerchief tucked into a pocket.

"It's that type of detail that's required in the turnout classes," Sarah said as she plucked a coin from the pocket of another jacket. "Some of the judges will even check to make sure you have a gold coin."

"That's so silly!" Amanda rolled her eyes. "A coin won't make the horses look or go any better."

"Most of it is tradition from hundreds of years ago," Sarah explained as she handed Vicki a brown tweed jacket, a cream stock and matching waistcoat, hand-stitched mustard jodhpurs, beige leather gloves and a velvet helmet to try on.

While Vicki headed to the bathroom to get changed, Kelly watched Sarah sorting through even more gear.

"I'm pretty sure this will fit Dandy," she said, holding up an elaborate gold, brown and orange show browband encrusted with hundreds of crystals. "My chestnut mare Fire and Ice used to wear it."

"It's beautiful," Kelly gasped, as it sparkled in the afternoon light.

Pulling an orange tie from the wardrobe, Sarah

held it out to Kelly for closer inspection. "This is the tie that belongs with it."

"How do I look?" Vicki asked, as she rejoined them. Kelly raised her eyebrows, hardly able to recognise her sister beneath all the smart clothing.

"You don't look real," Amanda blurted out.

"What do you mean?" Vicki frowned, shuffling her feet self-consciously.

"You look like one of the riders in the magazines," Amanda said, her face breaking into a wide smile. "I never thought people could look like that in real life."

"The outfit is perfect," Sarah said, approvingly. "I'll put it aside for you to wear at the show. You just need cufflinks and leather boots."

"Thank you so much," Vicki said shyly. "For the first time in my life I feel like I'll actually have all the proper gear. I just have one question — why does this outfit have a stock instead of a tie?"

"Because Koolio's a saddle hunter, and Dandy's a show pony."

Three blank faces stared back at Sarah.

"What's a saddle hunter?" Kelly asked.

"I keep forgetting you've never competed on the open classes at a national show before," Sarah said.

"The local shows have everyone in the same ring, but at the big shows they're split into two types. Saddle hunters are bigger-boned horses, and their saddlery is plainer. They're the type of horses you'd traditionally find on a hunt field. By comparison, show ponies are prettier and far more refined — they're the ones that are decked out in brighter colours and flashier browbands."

"So what's Magic?" Amanda asked as she tried to place her chunky Welsh pony.

"A saddle hunter for sure," Sarah said. "But it doesn't matter so much for you and Kelly, because all the show ponies and saddle hunters compete together for the rider and hunter classes."

"There's so many rules." Kelly's mind was struggling to keep track of everything Sarah had told them.

Glancing at her watch, Vicki gasped. "It's almost six. I'd better get changed so we can get home and feed the horses before dinner."

Chapter 17
Tricks of the Trade

THE NEXT FEW WEEKS were spent with Sarah building up to the competition. Not only was she teaching them how to ride intricate workouts, but she was also teaching them methods to catch the judges' eyes and stand out from the other riders. Even though they had a lot to learn in a very short time, the girls made sure to keep a good balance by riding out on the farm, too, so their ponies wouldn't become bored from too much schooling.

They also kept competing at the local shows. As Koolio gained experience in the ring, he quickly outshone his rivals and at several shows he was unbeaten, winning every class he and Vicki entered.

"He's come a long way from the problem pony I had to deal with those first couple of months," Kelly remarked, as she watched Koolio being awarded his first Supreme Champion on the Flat, just two weeks before the Royal Show.

"So have Dandy, Magic and Casper," Mum said proudly, putting her arm around her daughter's shoulders. "I'm so impressed by how much you girls have learnt."

"I can't believe all three of us won our rider classes today. That's the first time that's ever happened!"

"There were only two riders in your class," Mum laughed. "I'm not sure that counts."

"Of course it does," Kelly argued. "I could have come second!"

∪ ∪ ∪

With less than two weeks to go, Sarah arrived at the house with her arms laden with supplies.

Kelly glanced at the contents of the bags and

looked at Sarah sceptically. "What do we need all of this dye for?"

"Koolio's tail needs to be dyed black to match his mane, and Dandy needs to be a richer chestnut," Sarah said, as she began mixing colours.

"Are most of the show ponies dyed?" Vicki asked. She looked as if she was also unable to comprehend why their ponies weren't good enough in their natural state.

"It's the fakest discipline of them all," Sarah grinned, not seeming to mind the question. "Not only are many dyed, but people even paint on extra white socks to make their horses look like they have symmetrical markings. They use false manes and tails, too."

"It seems like a lot of effort to win a ribbon," said Kelly.

"Half the fun is seeing how much you can transform a horse to maximise its beauty."

"It kind of seems like cheating," Vicki said.

"Not at all. It's no different to other kinds of show business," Sarah reasoned. "People use makeup, fake nails, hair extensions and clothes to enhance their own beauty, too. You don't honestly think the models in the magazines wake up looking like that, do you?"

"Of course not," Kelly said, understanding dawning. "They spend ages doing their hair and makeup."

"It's the same with show ponies," Sarah explained. "I can guarantee none of those top ponies in the magazines look like that in the paddock either. A lot of effort behind the scenes has gone into their presentation."

"Our ponies never look that much different at shows," Kelly said.

"They will by the time I finish with them." Sarah winked. "I bet you'll barely recognise them."

They watched as Sarah coated all of Dandy's white markings with Vaseline so the dye wouldn't stain them. Then she carefully bandaged his legs in plastic wrap and began sponging the purple mixture onto his coat.

"He looks ridiculous," Kelly frowned once the dyeing was finished. His entire body was so dark he looked almost black.

"Most of that will wash out — he'll only end up one shade darker," Sarah reassured her. "Let's dye Koolio's tail while Dandy's dye sets."

The girls then watched with interest as Sarah filled a bucket with black dye, then applied it to the horse's tail, careful to stop Koolio flicking spatters over his white rump. The top of Koolio's tail was already black like his mane, knees and hocks, which contrasted with his white coat, so by the time they were finished there was no way anyone would ever guess it wasn't his real colour.

U U U

The finishing touches were added on the day of the show. Once again, the sisters watched in amazement as Sarah set to work turning out their ponies. Her nimble fingers flew as she plaited and sewed plaits into their manes, making each pony's plaits slightly different.

"Why have you made Magic's plaits so small?" Amanda asked, inspecting the tiny rosettes that lined her pony's crest.

"To give her the illusion of a longer neck," Sarah said. "And Dandy's are set slightly higher, to make his neck appear thicker."

"I didn't even know that was possible," Vicki said, overwhelmed by all the tips and tricks Sarah was sharing with them. Apart from brushing their ponies, she hadn't let them lift a finger to help.

"The tail's equally important," Sarah said, as she grabbed a chestnut and a black false tail from the truck and deftly plaited them into the base of Dandy and Koolio's docks. "The right length and thickness can make a horse's conformation look more balanced."

"What else has to be done?" Kelly asked, intrigued.

"Their features need to be darkened and their hooves blackened."

Kelly watched in shock as Sarah lifted each hoof and placed it on a square of carpet so she could paint it black. While she waited for each hoof to dry, she rubbed black oil into the ponies' knees and hocks, before rubbing makeup into their inner ears, onto their muzzles and around their eyes and cheekbones.

By the time Sarah was finished, there was no doubt the ponies looked exquisite, although Kelly felt a little saddened that she could barely recognise them. Dandy looked especially different, now a deep red chestnut rather than his usual copper tones.

"The only thing left is to oil and buff them until their coats gleam." Sarah stood back to admire Koolio, Dandy and Magic. "But we'll wait until they're tacked up, so the oil doesn't cause the saddle to slip."

Chapter 18
Saddle Hunter Champion

Twenty minutes later, as Vicki sat on Koolio while Sarah polished the soles of her boots, Kelly couldn't contain a yawn. They'd been up since four that morning and it had taken every single minute of the past five hours to get their three ponies ready.

"Don't pat him — you'll get makeup all over you!" Sarah cried out, catching Amanda's hand just as it was stretching up to rub Koolio's head.

"I keep forgetting," Amanda groaned. "I'll be covered in black smudges by the end of the day!"

"Make sure you don't let your ponies rub their heads on you either," Sarah warned, as they followed Vicki to the ring. "I've ruined a lot of clothes that way over the years — the stains never wash out."

Amanda giggled. "What if the judge tries to pick up Koolio's legs and his hands come away black?"

"Luckily, the judges aren't allowed to touch the horses," Sarah laughed.

U U U

"Who's the grey?" Kelly overheard a glamorous woman asking from the sidelines as Koolio trotted out of the ring with a red ribbon tied around his graceful neck.

"I've never seen him before," her friend uttered. She took a sip from a glass of champagne and the bracelets on her arm tinkled.

"Neither have I," a third said sourly. "I can't believe our daughters just got beaten by a pony no one's ever heard of."

Moving hastily away from the rival mothers, Kelly walked over to congratulate her beaming sister.

"You've only done one class and already you've qualified for Champion," Mum said, reaching up to hug her daughter. "Koolio outclassed every pony in that ring."

"He's sure proved he belongs out there with the best of them." Vicki's eyes twinkled as she turned Koolio back towards the gate. "I'm in the next class, too, so I better hurry."

For the next hour, Kelly watched with bated breath as her sister entered the ring time and time again. Without fail she left with either a red or a blue ribbon around Koolio's neck.

"I've almost won enough prize money to refill your piggy bank," Vicki said, as she handed over yet another ribbon and envelope.

"It wouldn't have mattered if you hadn't," Kelly reassured her sister.

"They're judging Champion in five minutes," Sarah said, as she walked over a few minutes later with a bucket filled with brushes, makeup, oil and boot polish to freshen up both horse and rider. "Only two ponies have qualified."

"I've beaten her once, and she's beaten me once," Vicki said, as Sarah ran a rag over her riding boots, brushed out Koolio's tail and wiped his bit clean. "We're pretty evenly matched."

"It's anyone's game," Sarah nodded. She sprayed a final mist of oil on Koolio's gleaming hindquarters. "Ride him like you stole him."

Kelly burst into a fit of laughter. "She kind of did! Steal him, I mean."

Dad gave Kelly's hand a squeeze as Vicki entered the ring to contest the saddle hunter championship. "Do you regret trading him now?"

"No way," Kelly said, as she settled in the grass to watch Koolio face off against a beautiful black mare. "None of us would be here if I'd kept him. He certainly wouldn't be looking or performing like that if I was still riding him, that's for sure!"

"You wouldn't have won Reserve Champion at the A&P Show, either," Mum added, watching as Vicki guided Koolio through a picture-perfect workout — his gallop was flawless.

"I still can't believe the plaits lost you the Champion," Amanda said cheekily.

"In my mind it still counts as winning," Kelly said. She didn't care about the colour of the ribbon she had hanging on her wall.

As Vicki halted Koolio before the judge and bent her head in a salute, Sarah jumped up and down in excitement. "That's done it!" she said. "It's the best she's ever ridden."

"Don't count your chickens before they hatch," Dad cautioned, but his words were quickly drowned out as everyone jumped to their feet, cheering and hollering as the judge motioned Vicki forward. Kelly's face beamed with pride as the judge placed a wreath of purple and orange flowers around Koolio's neck, followed by a purple sash.

As music played out across the showgrounds Vicki circled the ring at a gallop, closely followed by the black mare, who carried a lilac ribbon and a scowling rider.

"She doesn't look very happy," Amanda said as they watched the other rider pass by. "I'd be grinning from ear to ear if I'd just won Reserve Champion!"

"They imported that mare from Australia a few months ago for twenty-five thousand dollars," Sarah said. "I'm pretty sure she's been undefeated until now."

"She'd be even more upset if she knew she'd been beaten by a pony that only cost a thousand dollars,

then," Dad said. It was hard to believe Vicki had taken top honours against such an expensive pony.

"He'd be worth ten times that now for sure," Sarah chuckled, as Mum pulled out her camera and snapped a photo of the victorious pair. "People will be talking about him all season."

Taking Koolio's reins, Kelly held him while her sister leapt to the ground and was wrapped up in a series of hugs. She felt so proud of Vicki and everything she had accomplished.

"From the moment I saw him, I had no doubt he'd be a champion one day," Kelly grinned as they led Koolio back to the truck, so they could all get ready for their rider classes. "I have to admit, though, I did imagine it would be me riding him."

"When I outgrow him, he'll be all yours again," Vicki said, holding out her hand to make a pinky promise. "And in the meantime, you've got Dandy. Now get out there and show them what you can do."

Koolio

Koolio was a 146-cm grey gelding, who was six years old when he joined our family in 2001. He was the most talented and successful ponies we owned in our early years of competition and it's only with hindsight that we have been able to appreciate how remarkable he was.

His versatility wowed the judges and he would come home from every show with plenty of ribbons.

Not only did he excel in the saddle hunter and hunter classes, but he also successfully competed in eventing, games, dressage competitions and Pony Club.

The adventures of Koolio will continue in the next two books in this series — *Pepe, the Beach Stallion* and *Jackamo, the Supreme Champion*.

Characters

Vicki has always shown talent for riding, training and competing with horses. She has won national titles and championships in Showing, Show Hunter and Show Jumping, and has represented New Zealand internationally. Dandy was the first pony she trained, when she was nine years old, and then twenty years later she won the World Championships for Colt Starting. When she's not riding, she loves to learn as much about horses as she can, from farriers, vets, physios and dentists.

Kelly has always been creative. She loves horses, photography and writing. Although she competed to Grand Prix level when she was sixteen, she now only show jumps for fun, and also enjoys taming wild horses. Her favourite rides are out on the farm, swimming in the river, or cantering down the beach. When she's not on a horse, she is very daring, and loves going on extreme adventures.

Amanda is the family comedian and can always make people laugh! As a child, she was always pulling pranks and getting up to mischief. Amanda began show jumping at a young age, and competed in her first Grand Prix when she was twelve. In 2010, she won the Pony of the Year, the most prestigious Pony Grand Prix in the Southern Hemisphere, and since then she has had lots of wins up to World Cup level. When she's not outside training her horses or teaching other riders, Amanda loves doing something creative — she has already filmed two documentaries, and is writing her first book.

Mum (Heather Wilson) grew up with a love of horses, although she was the only one in her family to ride. She volunteered at a local stable from the age of thirteen, teaching herself to ride when she was gifted an injured racehorse. Although she rides only occasionally now, her love of horses hasn't faded over the years, and she is always ringside to watch her daughters compete. In her spare time, Heather loves painting and drawing anything to do with horses, and as 'Camp Mum' is popular with the young riders who attend Showtym Camps.

Dad (John Wilson) grew up with horses, hunting, playing polo and riding on the farm. His family also show jumped and trained steeplechasers, so he has loved horses from a young age. He hurt his back when he was in his twenties, which has limited his horse riding, but he enjoys watching his daughters ride and is very proud of their success. When he's not fixing things around the farm, he can be found gardening or creating stunning life-sized horse sculptures from recycled horseshoes.

How-tos

The most important thing about owning a pony is to learn as much as you can about their care and training, so you can make their life as fun and easy as possible! In each book in the Showtym Adventures series, we will expand on key lessons Vicki, Amanda and I learnt on our journey to becoming better horse riders. Some lessons we learnt by making mistakes; others from observing our horses and learning from them — and some knowledge has been passed down to us by others. We hope you enjoy these top tips!

How to buy the perfect pony!

Buying a new pony is one of the most exciting things you can ever do, but it also can be a challenge to find one perfectly suited to you. Over the years, we've had hundreds of horses and ponies; some have been our dream ponies and others have been straight from our nightmares. There is nothing worse than working with a problem pony like Koolio if you don't have the skills to deal with them, and unfortunately, most people don't have an older sister like Vicki to help them out!

Below are some of our top tips for when you are looking for a new pony:

- Write a list of goals and dreams you'd like to achieve with your new pony — and what you enjoy most about riding. That way, you'll buy a horse suited to your favourite discipline, whether it be dressage, jumping, trekking or a general all-rounder.
- Be honest about your capabilities, and buy a pony suited to your level of confidence and experience; otherwise you risk losing your enjoyment of riding.
- Remember that bigger is not always better. Pick a pony

that is the right size and temperament for you now, not one you'll grow into several years down the track.

- Look over the horse's conformation, soundness and age to ensure it is suited for your purposes.
- Don't fall in love with the first pony you find. Try lots of ponies and compare their strengths and weaknesses before picking the one that feels right to you.
- Try your favourite a few times and in different locations; at a show, on the farm or beach, or at another arena to see how the pony behaves in unfamiliar environments.
- Ask a lot of questions about a pony, not only about its performance but how it handles and behaves to ensure it will be suited to you. It is always a good idea to ask for references and not just take the owner at their word.
- If you're looking for a competition pony, it is always a good idea to get a vet check and x-rays to ensure the horse is sound enough to compete. Hidden issues can limit a pony, or cause it to misbehave.
- If you're not experienced at shopping for a horse, take an instructor or a knowledgeable horse person with you to offer a second opinion.

How to help your pony settle into a new home

Once you've found a dream pony, it's important to settle your new pony into its new home. This can be a stressful and confusing time for your pony because they will be losing all their human and horsey friends and everything they know, and find themselves suddenly living with strangers. In many ways, it's like a foster kid who has to get used to new people and new rules every time they change homes.

Below are ways you can help your horse transition to a new home as smoothly as possible:

- If you're moving your pony to a new property even the grass and hay will be different. If you plan to change your new pony to hard feed or minerals, make sure you do it gradually over a few weeks. It may be helpful to feed your horse a toxin binder or give them a gastrointestinal product to prevent ulcers, which can develop from the stress of changing properties and feed.
- Be realistic in your goals and expectations of your new horse. Remember it takes about six months to develop a partnership with your horse and two years to truly get the best from them; don't expect perfection overnight.

- Make sure you have gear that correctly fits your pony, including a bridle, bit and saddle. A poorly fitted saddle can cause problems, so it is important to get the fit checked by a professional.
- Horses are herd animals so it's important they have other horses for company. Even if you don't own any other horses, having a paddock companion is important for your pony's wellbeing. When introducing new ponies, first let them sniff noses while they are on lead ropes, then paddock or yard them beside each other. Once they seem settled, you can turn your pony out into the paddock with one other horse. Then, gradually integrate your pony with other horses.
- Introduce any changes to their routine and training slowly — too much change at once in stressful for them.
- If your new pony changes its behaviour after arriving at your property, contact the previous owner to see if this is normal. If it isn't, try to find out what is causing the change in behaviour — it might be as simple as a change in routine, different feed, a recent injury or a poorly fitted saddle.

Glossary

A&P Show agricultural and pastoral fair with displays of
livestock and farming equipment, entertainment, food
stalls and competitions — including show jumping.

Arabian an ancient horse breed from the Arabian Peninsula,
known for their distinctive heads, speed and intelligence.

bit the metal mouthpiece of a bridle.

bridle gear placed on the horse's head — including the bit
and reins — that is used to direct and guide the animal.

browbands the strap on the bridle which goes over the
horse's brow or forehead. Browbands can be plain leather
or include bright decorations.

canter the horse gait between a trot and a gallop.

conformation a horse's conformation is judged to be good or
bad by analysing, amongst other things, their proportions,
bone structure and muscle definition. Conformation
depends on the breed of the horse and what they have
been bred for.

crossbars a simple horse jump with two horizontal crossbars
raised on two vertical posts. The height of the horizontal
crossbars can be adjusted according to how high a horse
can jump.

dairy a small grocery store.

dressage a form of horse training where horse and rider work together to learn a collection of particular movements — a bit like dance! In competitions, horses are judged on their balance, movement and obedience.

eventing a horse and rider compete across cross-country, show jumping and dressage against other horse and rider combinations.

farm a ranch where livestock are raised.

gallop the fastest horse gait.

gelding a castrated male horse.

girth a cinch, the band that secures the saddle to a horse.

Grand Prix show jumping the top level of show jumping.

halt to come to a stop.

halter a harness for a horse's head, used to lead the horse.

hunter class event a competition in which a horse and rider must navigate a course of fences.

jig-jog between a walk and a slow trot, a jig-jogging horse is very uncomfortable to ride. Horses jig-jog for a number of different reasons including anxiety or excitement.

lollies confectionery, candy.

mane the hair that grows on the top ridge of a horse's neck.

muzzle the nose and jaws of a horse.

paddock a pasture or field of grass where horses are kept.

pony small horse breeds that are under 14.2 hands tall.

reserve a section of land set aside for public use, a reservation.

Ribbon Day a day of competitions where ribbons are awarded as prizes to the winners.

Royal Easter Show an annual event held at Easter with carnival rides, agricultural events, live music, food stalls and sporting events.

saddlery another word for tack, the gear needed to ride a horse.

show jumping competitors take turns going over a set course which includes a variety of obstacles. The horse and rider are judged on their ability and also on their speed.

showing in this competition, a horse is judged on its physical features and how it moves. If a horse has good conformation it should appear elegant and its movements will be light and balanced.

spooky used to describe a horse that is skittish or uneasy.

tack horse equipment.

trek riding a pony or horse across country, also known as trail riding.

trot the gait between a walk and a canter.

truck a horse truck, a vehicle and horse carrier in one.

walk the slowest horse gait.

woolshed a large shed on a farm, used for shearing sheep.

Thank you

WRITING THE *SHOWTYM ADVENTURES* SERIES fills me with nostalgia; not only for our childhood, but for a way of life that is slowly being lost. Growing up, we didn't have televisions, cell phones or wireless internet, but we had active imaginations and the world was our playground. I hope these stories inspire you to head outside and make your own adventures.

While there were times we were completely feral, thanks to the mentorship of people like Anna Paratene (who inspired the character Sarah) we also learnt how to polish our rough edges and present ourselves professionally in the show ring. Anna's time as a show judge and the kindness she showed us in sharing her skills have stood us in good stead over the years. While we predominantly show jump, we still occasionally compete in the show ring; the last time was in 2011 when Vicki won Saddle Hunter and Working Hunter championships at the Horse of the Year Show on her showjumper Showtym Commodore, as well as winning the turnout prize.

To this day our horses are very versatile and have a diverse life, just like Koolio and the rest of our ponies had. At our cores, we are still those same fun-loving children. Our top horses have epic adventures: cattle mustering, galloping down the beach and swimming in the river. Life is not designed to be routine, and horses aren't born to live in stables or be ridden solely on arenas. I truly believe it's our job to offer our equine partners some freedom and fun, and we also owe it to ourselves. Life is supposed to be a grand adventure and I am thankful to my family and our horses for constantly reminding us to enjoy the small things in life and make the most of every moment.

Besides Anna, there are so many other equestrians who have challenged us and taught us over the years. You've already met a few of them in previous books in this series, and you'll meet more in the coming books. No matter how big or small their part was in our journey, they have been remembered for a good reason. Every bit of knowledge we have has come from somewhere; learnt either from the horses we've owned or ridden, or from a person who crossed our path. So thank you — we value the time and knowledge you shared with us and strive to pay it forward with the riders we mentor today.

Of course the people that influence us the most are the ones we see on a daily basis, so the biggest thanks must go to my parents and sisters. We have woven a great life together filled with enough adventures and memories to last a lifetime.

DID YOU ENJOY THIS BOOK?

We love hearing from readers! Here's what some of you have told us about the *Showtym Adventures* series.

"My favourite books are *Showtym Adventures* by Kelly Wilson. My favourite book out of the series is *Cameo, the Street Pony*. My favourite part in the book is when they find Cameo." — Evie

"Yesterday I went and bought *Cameo, the Street Pony*. I couldn't put it down and finished it in a day. It is an amazing story on how to overcome fear, and the journey it takes you on is overall amazing. I love how Kelly has her list and Vicki is more than happy to help (although Amanda's cheekiness is some of the best)! I cannot wait for the next book and Kelly's books just keep on getting better and better." — Rylee

"I'm 11 years old. Nana bought me the book about Vicki's story of *Dandy, the Mountain Pony* . . . on the 2nd chapter I was picturing about what was happening and I hope that I follow in your footsteps with horses." — Evelyn

"I absolutely loved it to pieces. It has inspired me that girls can do anything and dreams really can come true if you want them to. It was a fantastic book. I would rate it 1,000,000,000,000,000,000,000,000,000, stars and even more! Please make more books because I am very excited for the next one." — Augustine

ABOUT THE AUTHOR

© Kelly Wilson

Kelly Wilson is an award-winning photographer and designer, and the bestselling author of four non-fiction books, *For the Love of Horses, Stallion Challenges, Mustang Ride* and *Saving the Snowy Brumbies*; a picture book, *Ranger the Kaimanawa Stallion*; and the *Showtym Adventures* series. With her sisters Vicki and Amanda, Kelly has starred in the hit-rating TV series, *Keeping up with the Kaimanawas*, following their work taming New Zealand's wild Kaimanawa horses, and has travelled to America and Australia to rescue and tame wild horses.

www.kellywilson.nz

Have you read . . . Book 1 in the
Showtym Adventures **series?**

DANDY, THE MOUNTAIN PONY

Let the adventure begin . . . taming a WILD pony!

When nine-year-old Vicki Wilson's beloved lease pony is sold, she is heartbroken. Her family doesn't have much money, and she is desperate to have a pony of her own so she can keep riding.

Then Vicki has the chance she has been waiting for, to tame and train her own wild pony! How will she earn the trust of her beautiful new chestnut? And will Dandy ever be quiet enough for her to ride at Pony Club or compete at Ribbon Days?

This book is inspired by the Wilson Sisters' early years, where Vicki, Kelly and Amanda Wilson first encounter horses in the wild and learn what it takes to make them into champions.

Have you read . . . Book 2 in the
Showtym Adventures series?

CAMEO, THE STREET PONY

The adventure continues . . . training a street pony into a show pony!

When nine-year-old Kelly Wilson outgrows her pony, her mum surprises her with a beautiful steel-grey mare that she spotted trotting down the street, tied to the back of a truck. But there's a catch. Cameo has never been ridden!

While her sisters Vicki and Amanda are jumping higher than ever before, Kelly must face her fears on an untested pony. Will Cameo ever be ready for competitions? And will the girls' ponies hold their own against the purebreds at the Royal Show?

This exciting story of setbacks and success, in which Vicki, Kelly and Amanda Wilson first experience the thrill of serious competition, is inspired by the Wilson Sisters' early years.

Have you read . . . Book 3 in the
Showtym Adventures series?

CASPER, THE SPIRITED ARABIAN

Vicki's biggest challenge yet . . . to transform a dangerous pony!

When Vicki hears about a difficult Arabian that no one wants, she will stop at nothing to save him. Years of misunderstanding have left Casper wayward and mistrustful, but Vicki senses a gentle soul beneath the pony's rough exterior.

Vicki must learn the importance of patience and compromise to have any chance of winning over the high-strung gelding. Will Casper ever trust humans again? And will Vicki be able to uncover the potential she sees in the spirited Arabian?

This story of self-discovery and second chances, in which Vicki, Kelly and Amanda Wilson first help a misunderstood pony to trust again, is inspired by the Wilson Sisters' early years.

Have you read . . . Book 4 in the
Showtym Adventures series?

CHESSY, THE WELSH PONY

Diamonds in the rough . . . will these unwanted ponies find love?

Seven-year-old Amanda Wilson dreams of training her own wild pony, just as her big sisters have done. Then comes the chance — a muster of beautiful Welsh ponies that have run wild in the hills.

Among them is Chessy, a striking stallion, and just the right size for Amanda. But small doesn't equal easy, and first Amanda must prove she has what it takes by training Magic, a stroppy mare from Pony Club. Will Magic and Chessy ever be safe enough to join Amanda on her crazy adventures?

Vicki and Kelly must help Amanda to win her ponies' trust in this engaging story of perseverance and reward, which is inspired by the Wilson Sisters' early years.

Coming next . . . Don't miss Book 6 in the
Showtym Adventures series

PEPE, THE BEACH STALLION

It's a whole new world . . . rescuing and rehabilitating an injured stallion!

When Vicki and her sisters discover horses roaming on country roads because the locals can't afford fences to contain them, their eyes are opened to a whole new world of hardship.

Then Vicki meets Pepe, once a prized beach-racing stallion now crippled by mistreatment. Convinced the beaten horse will die, the owners agree to sell him. Will Vicki be able to save the injured racer? And will Pepe accept his new life after galloping at full speed?

This story of hope and redemption is inspired by the Wilson Sisters' early years.